Also by Maurine F. Dahlberg

Play to the Angel
The Spirit and Gilly Bucket
Escape to West Berlin

THE STORY OF JONAS

MAURINE F. DAHLBERG

THE STORY OF JONAS

Farrar Straus Giroux / New York

The author gratefully acknowledges
Dr. John David Smith, Charles H. Stone
Distinguished Professor of American History,
the University of North Carolina at Charlotte,
for his critical reading of the manuscript.

www.fsgkidsbooks.com

Library of Congress Cataloging-in-Publication Data
Dahlberg, Maurine F., date.
    The story of Jonas / Maurine F. Dahlberg.— 1st ed.
        p.   cm.
    Summary: In the mid-1800s, a slave boy dreams of escaping to freedom
while on a journey from Missouri to the gold fields of Kansas Territory with
his master's n'er-do-well son.
    ISBN-13: 978-0-374-37264-4
    ISBN-10: 0-374-37264-0
    [1. Slavery—Fiction.   2. Fugitive slaves—Fiction.   3. African Americans—
Fiction.   4. Voyages and travels—Fiction.]   I. Title.

PZ7.D15157 St 2007
[Fic]—dc22

                                                            2006041344

In memory of my longtime friend Mary Scott Webb

THE STORY OF JONAS

1

JONAS EASED OFF HIS HURTFUL SHOES AND WIGGLED HIS toes up and down. His feet ached from being squeezed so tight, and they had been pricked where the shoe nails stuck through the stiff leather. But Master William and Miz Julia liked for their house servants here at Split Oak Farm to dress fancy, and those were the only shoes Jonas had. One pair of shoes a year, that was what slaves got.

"Jonas, time to eat!" called Esther from the kitchen below.

"Be there in a minute!" he hollered back down. "Just taking off my good clothes."

Esther was the Hoopers' cook. Jonas helped her in the kitchen, and he helped Leola, the house girl, clean the Big House and wait on the Hoopers. Leola was about his age, thirteen or so, and she and her older brother, Tate, who worked in the hemp fields, were Jonas's friends.

Esther had worked in the hemp fields, too, until last fall, when Jonas's mama, who had been the cook, died of the cholera. Esther wasn't nearly as good a cook as Mama had been, but she got in a huff if Jonas told her how Mama would have done something. "That ain't the way *I* does it," she would answer stubbornly. So, because Jonas liked her, he tried to keep quiet.

Every time Jonas pictured Mama's sweet face, he still felt as if a powerful hand were wringing his heart, squeezing out more tears than he'd have thought a heart could hold. Each day he visited her grave, out behind the field hands' cabins. Her gravestone was a flat rock from down by the Blackwater River, etched with what he guessed said Nancy, her name, and 1858, her burying year. He'd sit beside that rock and talk to Mama, and it would bring him comfort.

Jonas's daddy had died, too, long ago, but his grave was on Master William's daddy's farm, Hooper Hall, which was down the road a piece. Daddy had had to stay there when Mama and Jonas had been sent here to Split Oak Farm. Jonas reckoned that if Daddy's grave had a stone, it would say Ben and the date he died, about eight years ago. Jonas had accompanied Master William to Hooper Hall several times, but he'd never had the courage to ask if someone would take him to Daddy's grave. He hoped he could visit it someday so he could say, Remember me, your little Jonas that you used to carry round on your shoulders? I'm near growed-up now, but I ain't forgot you. I still love you and Mama.

Esther called impatiently, "You coming, Jonas? We gotta eat so's we can wash the dishes."

"Coming!" Everything at Split Oak Farm was hurry, hurry, on account of there being so much work to do. Split Oak Farm wasn't large, but it was one of the best hemp farms in Saline County, Missouri. Master William was strict about how his hemp was grown and prepared, and buyers knew it would make strong rope and sturdy bagging for cotton bales. The field hands were kept busy year round, planting, raising, cutting, drying, and breaking apart the tough hemp plants, and the house servants had to wait on the commission men, bankers, and merchants who often came to call.

Jonas took off his white table-waiting shirt and folded it carefully on his cornshuck mattress. Then he went down the narrow, winding steps, wearing just his britches.

Esther was dishing up chicken stew out of a cast-iron pot that hung from a crane over glowing coals on the hearth. As Jonas came in, she turned around. "Honey, what you trying to do, get pneumonia? Ain't even May yet, and you running around without no shirt on!"

"It be almost May, and plenty warm." Jonas took the steaming bowl of stew she gave him, carried it to the work-table, and sat down on a cane-bottom chair.

Esther brought her bowl and settled across from him, her chair creaking a complaint. It was used to Jonas's dainty mama, not to big, fat Esther.

Esther was stout and had light-hued skin, the color of walnut shells. Jonas was small, like Mama, and his skin was as dark and glossy as chestnuts. He was darker than Mama had been—more like Daddy. Mama had always said he had Daddy's wide grin, too. It pleased him, knowing he took after both his parents. It made him feel that they were still alive, through him.

He lifted the blue towel that covered the bread basket, but only crumbs met his eye.

"Ain't no more bread," Esther said. "Them folks in the Big House done et it all. They sure can eat. Ain't much left when they gets finished."

"I forgot, Master Percy ate the last of the bread." Jonas sighed. "He eat like a prize hog. At supper, he had four slices of bread, three bowls of stew, and half the apple pie."

"Lordy." Esther shook her head. "That man gonna eat up all we got in the larder."

Jonas told her, "He ain't no joy to wait on, neither. Thinks I ain't nothing but a set of hands and feet, put on Earth to fetch and tote for him."

Master Percy was the Hoopers' grown-up son. None of the servants liked him, and his mama and daddy didn't seem to know what to do with him. He'd failed in school, couldn't keep a job, and didn't take to farming. He gambled and drank, and had no-account friends. He wasn't even comely to look at. Like Jonas, he'd gotten his looks from both his parents, but in his case the result was unfortunate: with his mama's narrow face, long, bony nose, and light brown hair, and his daddy's pale gray eyes, he looked like a fish.

Last month Master Percy had lost another job—a nice one that his daddy had gotten him in the nearby town of Boonville, filing papers in a lawyer's office. Jonas and Leola knew he had lost it because they heard Master William hollering at him in the parlor. Master William hollered so loud that they giggled, saying probably the whole state of Missouri could hear him. But they stopped giggling when they found out that, without a job, Master Percy could no longer pay the rent at his Boonville board-inghouse and had talked his parents into letting him move back here to Split Oak Farm.

During his visits, Jonas and Leola had come to hate Master Percy. He was bearable when his mama and daddy were watching, but once he was out of their sight he be-came arrogant and cruel. He ordered the two house ser-vants around and jerked them by the arms. He cuffed Jonas on the back of the head, and he pinched Leola in places where he oughtn't to be pinching a gal.

"Thank the Lord he'll be leaving soon," Esther said. "Master William agreed to pay his way out to them gold fields, didn't he? Ain't that what you and Leola said?"

Jonas explained, "Master William agreed to pay his way, but only if Master Percy goes with folks he approves of. And they ain't found nobody yet."

Master Percy had been talking about those gold fields since last fall. At first Leola, Esther, and Jonas had nearly laughed their heads off. Imagine thinking you could dig up gold pieces the way you'd dig up beets or potatoes!

How could Master Percy be so foolish? But it turned out that the fields were real. The newspapers had stories, which he read aloud at the dinner table, about the many thousands of people at the gold fields and the gold they were finding. He had bought guidebooks and maps that said how to get there.

Then one day Master Percy had gotten an invitation to go with two friends. Jonas remembered how excited he was when he came to the dinner table and announced, "Dag and Bud are going to the gold fields, and they want me to come along!"

But for once Master William was firm with his son. "No, Percy, you are not going with the Chalmers brothers—not if you want me to pay for your trip. Those two boys are troublemakers. If you go, it will be with somebody mature and trustworthy—somebody who doesn't drink or gamble or take crazy chances. I'll ask my acquaintances. Perhaps one of them knows someone who's going and would take you along for a fee."

Now Esther stood up and stretched. "Well, I sure hope Master Percy go away soon, whether it be to the gold fields or to the Devil." She looked at Jonas. "You done eating?"

Jonas nodded, his mouth full. Together, the two of them carried the kettle of hot water from the fireplace over to the worktable, filled the dish-washing and dish-rinsing pans, and hung the half-full kettle back over the fire. Jonas wasn't fond of dish washing, but he knew he wouldn't be doing it forever. Last winter Master William had called him into his study and told him some exciting news.

"Now that I am getting older and the farm is doing so well, I've decided I will soon need a manservant," he'd said. "I think you have the makings of one. When it's time, I'll send you to Hooper Hall to learn from my father's manservant, Ebenezer."

"Yes, sir." Jonas had said it quietly and calmly, because that was how servants were supposed to speak. But if he hadn't restrained himself, a happy yell would have worked its way up his throat, and his feet would have started to dance. "Sir? When you reckon it be time?"

The master had pursed his lips and drummed his fingers on his desk, considering. Then he'd grabbed a pencil, stood up, and walked to the door. "Come and stand over here with your back against the wall. Stand up straight and hold still."

Jonas had stood there, hardly breathing. Master William had drawn a short pencil line right above his head, looked at it, and drawn another line above that one.

"When you get this tall," he'd said, pointing to the top line, "you'll be ready."

The second line was about half a thumb's length above the first one. Jonas had thought, Why, it won't take no time to grow that much! But now the snow had melted and the trees were misty-looking with green buds, and he hadn't grown at all. He checked every week when no one was watching. The only way he could reach that line was to stand on his tiptoes, and he knew Master William wouldn't let him do that when measuring time came.

But *some*day he'd reach that line. It made him smile to think about it. A manservant was as high up the ladder as a slave boy could dream of getting. He'd wear a fine suit, and sleep on a pallet in the master's bedroom. He'd lay out Master William's clothes, greet visitors, and be trusted with family secrets. He'd probably have a little boy, maybe Jigsy, to run errands for him. Best of all, he'd have been trained by Ebenezer. The straight-backed, grizzle-headed old man was the perfect manservant—dignified, discreet, loyal, and smooth-tongued. Jonas watched him admiringly whenever he accompanied Master William to Hooper Hall.

Jonas was drying the big serving bowl, dreaming about being Master William's manservant, when he heard quick footsteps coming down the pathway from the Big House. The kitchen door creaked open and Leola came in. Her dark eyes were big with worry in her thin, tan face.

"Jonas, Master William want to see you."

"He want to see *me*? Why?"

"Don't know. He just say fetch you. He be in the parlor with Master Percy."

Jonas's mind raced. What could the master want with him so sudden-like?

"Do Master look happy?" Esther asked Leola.

"Not unless having his mouth frowning down to his chin mean happy."

A chill went through Jonas. "You think I be in trouble?"

She shrugged helplessly. "Ain't got no idea. When I took them tea earlier, they was talking about Master Percy going to them gold fields. I don't know how your name got brought up, though. Now come on! The master don't like to wait."

"I—I got to go upstairs and put on my shirt and shoes."

Jonas ran upstairs, threw his ruffled white shirt over his head, jammed his feet into his shoes, and hobbled down the steps, still tucking his shirt into his pants.

Esther clasped his arm. "Honey, keep your eyes down and your voice low. Don't do nothing to anger nobody."

"I be all right," Jonas assured her. But he was trembling as he and Leola went out the door and up the walk to the Big House. Master William seldom whipped his people, but he did other things that hurt, such as thumping their heads against the wall, pulling and twisting their ears, and, worst of all, switching their legs with his riding crop.

Leola said hesitantly, "I reckon I could tell Master William I couldn't find you nowheres. Maybe he'd forget what it was he wanted."

"No, I'll go in," Jonas replied. Then, because they both knew that such a fib could get her a switching, he added, "But thank you kindly."

As they went up the walkway to the Big House, music, sweet and haunting, drifted up from the cabins. That was Tate, playing his reed flute. Tate had been moody lately, but he still played that flute like an angel come down from heaven. With all his heart, Jonas wished he could sit out here on the porch with Leola and listen to Tate's music instead of having to go see Master William.

When Leola opened the back door of the Big House, it swung smoothly and silently. The floorboards of the hallway shone, and the candles flickered brightly through their clean glass chimneys. Leola and Jonas did a good job of keeping the Big House nice, and they were proud of it.

Surely, thought Jonas, Master William ain't found fault with my work.

The two padded quietly to the parlor doorway.

"I be waiting outside," Leola whispered.

Jonas smiled at her, grateful.

Master William looked up and saw them. "Come in, Jonas. Leola, you may go."

He was sitting in the upholstered chair by the fireplace, his back as straight as a board and his hands in his lap. Jonas glanced up long enough to see that his bushy gray eyebrows were drawn together and his mouth looked as though he'd just sipped vinegar.

Master Percy slouched in another chair, sulking. His lanky hair hung down around his face, and he picked at a fingernail. Like his daddy, he wore a white linen shirt, good wool britches, and costly black boots.

Seeing those boots, Jonas thought, Huh! Ain't no nails pricking *their* feet.

Master William beckoned. "Come here."

Jonas walked over to Master William, his head bent. He told himself, Try to act dignified, like a manservant. Act like old Ebenezer. Keep your eyes down and speak softly. If he hurts you, just set your jaw and don't howl or whimper.

Master William said briskly, "I have a job for you to do."

"Yes, sir?" Jonas felt light-headed with relief. He wasn't in trouble, after all!

"My son is going on a trip out West. You'll be going with him."

"Sir?" Jonas was so startled that he almost looked Master William in the face. He caught himself and lowered his eyes before the master noticed.

"You'll be going to the gold fields with my son and about twenty more men. You'll cook for Percy and two others—the wagon train leader and a doctor. You'll also do their laundry, build the campfires, help drive the oxen, and do any other chores you're assigned." He hesitated. "As I recall, you can do all those things. You light the kitchen fire in the mornings, and help cook the meals. You've helped old Susie with the laundry, and you drove the oxen when Elijah was sick last year in plowing time. Am I right?"

"Yes, sir."

Master William gave a nod. "Good. You'll leave on May seventh. That's a week from Saturday."

He'd leave in less than two weeks! In a small voice, Jonas asked, "Sir? How far we going on this trip?"

"The gold fields are about eight hundred miles from here."

"Eight hundred miles, sir?"

Master Percy snorted and looked up from his fingernail-picking. "Oh, Papa, that doesn't mean anything to a slave boy. Think of it this way, Jonas. The church is a mile from here and Hooper Hall is four miles. We're going *eight hundred* miles. Now, what do you make of that?" He sat back, looking smug.

"I—I don't know, sir." The numbers hopped around in Jonas's head like crickets. He wasn't even certain how much a hundred was. He was sure of his numbers only up to twelve. Twelve let him read the clock and measure a foot. Twelve was a dozen, and anything higher was a-dozen-and-one and so on, up to two dozen. But how many dozens did it take to make eight hundred?

"Can't puzzle it out, can you, boy?" Master Percy laughed. Gleaming in the lamplight, his teeth looked small and sharp. A fish with coyote teeth, Jonas thought.

"Stop teasing him," Master William said. "Jonas, it will take six weeks or so to reach the gold fields. Depending on how lucky my son is at gold-digging, you will be gone about a year."

"A *year*, sir?" Surely Jonas had heard wrong!

"Yes, a year."

Jonas felt weak, and there was a funny buzzing in his ears. "But, sir—"

The master waved a hand in dismissal. "That's all. You may go now. And, Jonas . . ."

"Sir?"

He smiled slightly. "Perhaps when you get home you'll be tall enough to reach that pencil mark."

"Yes, sir." At least that would be something to look forward to during the long, unimaginable year to come.

2

THE REST OF THE EVENING WAS A BLUR OF TEARS AND talk and Esther's soothing herb tea. Jonas tried to take in the idea that he was leaving home for a year to go eight hundred miles to help Master Percy dig up gold pieces, but it seemed fantastical.

Finally the women went home to the slave quarters. Leola shared a cabin with two field hands, Agatha and Carrie, and Esther lived with her man, Nestor, and her grandson Jigsy.

Jonas climbed the steps to his room in the kitchen attic, where he'd moved after Mama had died. He lay on his thin cornshuck mattress and wondered about the trip he would take. What sights would they see? Would people look and act and talk like the people at home? Would there be other black folks? Would they meet Indians? How would they get food and drink? Where would they sleep?

Would they be in danger? Would they see wild animals? Did the sun and moon shine overhead in the West?

But in the following days, Master Percy and his daddy never mentioned the trip to Jonas. He thought, Guess they figure I be too dumb to have any questions in my head. All he knew was what he overheard: the gold fields were in Kansas Territory, near a mountain called Pikes Peak. First they would go on a steamboat to a place called Kansas City, where they would join the wagon train. Their leader was a man named Jeremiah Quincy. He had once hauled freight on the Santa Fe Trail, which they would take most of the way. Mr. Quincy and his friend, a widowed doctor named Henry Yoder, were going to the gold fields together. They had agreed to share their wagon with Master Percy in return for Jonas's cooking. When the men finished digging for gold, Mr. Quincy and the doctor would go on to California, where they aimed to live out their days, and Master Percy would find another party that he and Jonas could return with.

"But not those Chalmers boys," Master William told his son sternly.

Master Percy scowled. "Aw, Papa, you never did like Dag and Bud."

"And I never will," his father retorted. "I don't want you consorting with them on this trip. Understand?"

Master Percy grinned. "You needn't worry. I'll find so much gold I'll take a stagecoach home. Why, I'll find so much gold, I'll *buy* a stagecoach."

His father grunted.

Then one evening, Jonas learned something interesting from Tate.

Sometimes, after their work was finished, he, Leola, and Tate would sit on the ground behind the cabins, near Mama's burying place, and talk. They missed the days when they had worked together at youngsters' chores: sweeping the yard, gathering the eggs, and toting water to the field hands. Back then, they had talked and played together while they were working. Now they couldn't talk in private unless they came out here in the evenings and spoke too softly for anybody to hear.

When Jonas began telling them about his trip, Leola asked questions and added bits of information she had overheard. But Tate seemed to have his thoughts elsewhere. He just sat there with his arms wrapped around his knees, watching them chatter. Then, when Jonas mentioned where the gold fields were, Tate perked up. "That where you going, Kansas Territory?" he asked.

Surprised, Jonas nodded. "You heard of it?"

Tate smiled mysteriously. "Oh, I heard of it. It got something besides gold. Something better than gold."

"What?" asked Jonas warily. He didn't like the sly way his friend was talking.

Out of habit, Tate glanced around to make sure nobody could hear. When he spoke, it was in a whisper barely louder than the evening breeze. "It got freedom."

"Tate!" Leola whispered urgently. "What you saying?"

"I'm saying that if slaves get to Kansas Territory, they

be free," he said. "You know that field hand Richard from Hooper Hall? He been telling me about it."

Richard was one of several hands sent to Split Oak Farm to help with the spring planting. Master William didn't like him — said he was surly and uppity.

"But even if they be free, their masters can go across the border and snatch them back," Leola said vehemently. "I heard the master and missus talking about it."

"Their masters can't snatch them back if they can't find them. There's people — white people — in Kansas Territory that'll hide slaves. They're called . . ." Tate paused. "Abolitionists. They'll help slaves get up to Canada, where ain't *no*body can snatch them back. Jonas, this is your chance to get to freedom!"

Jonas shook his head. "I don't know, Tate."

"You want to be a slave all your life?" Tate snapped.

"No, course not, but — well, things ain't bad here. I got friends, a warm place to sleep, a job that ain't hard, and a master that like me. He even gonna make me his —"

"I know, his *man*servant." Tate turned and spat on the ground. "Sound like they be turning you into a white boy up there at that Big House. That what they doing?"

"Tate, stop!" hissed Leola. "Jonas ain't no white boy. But he ain't no fool, neither."

Jonas said, "Don't you know what happen if you get caught escaping? You get chewed up by the slave-hunting dogs, or tied to a tree and whipped, or sold South to sweat out your life in the cotton fields. No, sir, it ain't worth the chance, not to me."

Tate shrugged. "Reckon it be your decision."

"Tate—" started Leola.

He turned to her fiercely. "Don't you remember how the white folks killed our mama and daddy? Sent them to the field, not caring that they was sick with the fever. Then they sold us on the auction block. You forgot that?"

"No, I ain't forgot. But it weren't the Hoopers that done that," Leola protested.

"Don't matter. White folks is all the same." Tate stood up. "I be going on to bed."

He strode away. Jonas and Leola called after him as loudly as they dared, but the only reply they got was the sound of his cabin door shutting.

The rest of that week zipped by like a rabbit with hound dogs on its tail. On Wednesday, Miz Julia came out to the kitchen and queried Jonas about his chores so she could decide who would do them while he was gone. She was kindlier than Master William—slower to scold or punish—and he didn't mind answering her questions.

After she had talked to him, she tapped her pencil on her pad of paper. "You do a lot of work, Jonas. I may have to make Mr. Hooper get us a new boy."

Jonas's heart leaped. Maybe Master William couldn't afford a new servant, and he'd get to stay home! But then Esther, who was fixing soup, came over and said, "Begging your pardon, ma'am, but my grandson Jigsy can take on the work."

Miz Julia brightened. "Yes, I suppose he can. Then

when Jonas gets home, he can start his training as Mr. Hooper's manservant."

So that was settled.

Thursday afternoon, while the master and mistress were out, Jonas was scrubbing the hall floor. Master Percy bellowed from the parlor, "Jonas, come in here!"

Hastily Jonas wrung out his sponge and wiped his hands dry on his pants. In the parlor, he found Master Percy sprawled in Master William's favorite chair, holding a thick cigar stub in one hand. "Listen here, boy," he said, looking down his long nose. "On Saturday my papa will take us to Arrow Rock to catch the steamboat up the Missouri River to Kansas City. You'll need to be ready to go right after breakfast, with your goodbyes said and your things packed. There won't be any dawdling. Understand?"

"Yes, sir."

"One more thing," Master Percy added. "When we get to the Rockies, any gold pieces you find belong to me."

"Yes, sir."

"Don't forget it, or I'll whip you from here to kingdom come." He gestured with his cigar, flicking ashes on Miz Julia's carpet. "Well? Quit standing around, and get back to work!"

Jonas left quickly. He wished he'd had the courage to ask, What's Arrow Rock? Is a steamboat safe? What should I pack? What does a gold piece look like? But Master Percy probably would have jumped up and swatted him for being impudent. Jonas thought, That man will be downright intolerable once we leave here and his mama and daddy ain't around no more.

On Friday, Miz Julia gave Jonas one of the stout linen flour sacks she'd sewn, to carry his belongings in. He, Esther, and Leola tried to think what a person might need out West, but it was too baffling, so he figured he would just take all his belongings. They didn't amount to much: three shirts and two pairs of pants; his shoes, his straw hat, and some underthings; and his winter coat. The coat was Esther's idea. "Don't forget, you be gone a whole year," she reminded him. "Reckon wherever you be, it get cold come wintertime."

That night, all of the Hoopers' people—field hands and house servants—threw a party in Jonas's honor. It was the finest party he could remember. Everybody wore fancy churchgoing clothes. The men had laid a wood floor in an empty cabin for dancing on, and had built a long table to hold the food. Master William had donated a hog to roast, and Esther had fixed fried catfish, sweet potatoes, black-eyed peas, custards, and two apple pies. The field hands provided the music: Elijah played the banjo and Big Jim the fiddle. There weren't any drums, but the bare feet tapping and stomping on the floor pounded out the rhythm.

Best of all, when Tate came, he clapped Jonas on the back and joshed with him, acting more relaxed than he had for a long time. He even brought his flute, to entertain folks while Elijah and Big Jim rested. Instead of the odd tunes that he made up for himself, he played pieces that everyone knew: work songs they sang in the field, hymns about the joys of heaven, and melodies that drifted down from Miz Julia's piano when the parlor windows were open.

While Jonas was outside getting some fresh air, Tate came up and whispered, "Don't pay no mind to what I said the other night. I was just fired up. Didn't mean nothing."

"I sure am happy to hear that," Jonas said, relieved.

The dancing went on till all hours. Finally Esther tapped Jonas on the shoulder. "That's enough high-stepping and fancy-footing from you. If you don't go get some sleep, you be falling off that steamboat into the river come tomorrow."

Jonas protested, but he knew she was right, and said his farewells. Later, as he drifted off to sleep in his attic room, he could still hear the fiddle playing.

The next morning after breakfast, Jonas went to visit Mama's grave one last time. He whispered goodbye to Mama and hurried back to the kitchen. The Hoopers' wagon was already waiting in the front drive.

After Jonas had gotten his flour sack from the attic, Esther and Leola walked with him to the front drive. He hugged Esther and she whispered, "No matter what Master Percy do, you try to please him. If you don't, you just be making trouble for your own self."

Jonas nodded miserably.

Master Percy hollered, "Come on, boy! It's time to go!"

Miz Julia walked Jonas to the wagon. "Be a good boy," she said. "Say your prayers and strive to do the Lord's will. Ask Him to give you patience and strength for the hardships you must endure."

"Yes'm," Jonas replied. He thought, Her son gonna be the biggest hardship of all.

He climbed up into the wagon, sat down in the back, and put his flour sack beside his bare feet. He had hardly gotten settled when Master William clucked to the matched pair of bay horses and they started off. Miz Julia, Leola, and Esther waved to Jonas and the two men until they reached the end of the drive. They turned left and passed the old, lightning-damaged oak tree that gave the farm its name. When they passed the hemp fields, the field hands were gathered around Jigsy and the water bucket, taking a break. Jonas saw Tate standing off a ways, talking to a slight-built man with dull-black skin. Richard! Jonas didn't like seeing them together. But Tate had seemed all right at the party, Jonas reminded himself. Besides, he'd heard Master William say that Richard and the other borrowed field hands were going back to Hooper Hall today.

The men were silent and straight-backed in the front seat. The only sound was the clip-clop of the horses' hooves. Jonas dozed, worn out from last night's party.

He had thought Arrow Rock would be a big rock, maybe with an arrow painted on it, but it was a town up on a bluff. Master William didn't drive into town, though; he drove straight down to the steamboat landing. A number of men and several families with children were already there, waiting for the boat.

The Hoopers and Jonas climbed down from the wagon. Master William paid two strong-looking black men to haul Master Percy's trunks down to the riverside. Slipping them extra coins, he said, "Make sure they get loaded on the boat."

"Yes, sir!" the men replied, grinning and tugging respectfully at their straw hats.

After they had taken the trunks, Master William shook hands with his son. "Good luck to you, Percy. Write us when you get to Denver."

"I will, Papa. Take care of yourself and Mama."

Then Master William turned to Jonas and said, "Be a good boy, Jonas, and look after my son."

"Yes, sir."

Without saying more, Master William climbed back up onto the wagon seat and clucked to the horses. Jonas felt his eyes fill with tears. That wagon was his last link with home.

When the boat, the *Minnehaha*, pulled in, Master Percy made sure that his trunks got put on board and then motioned for Jonas to follow him up the ramp. "Hurry along, you black imp!" he snapped. "You want us to get left behind?"

There didn't seem much danger of that, since the deckhands still had several wagons, four horses, ten or so oxen, a flock of chickens, and a pile of baggage to load, but Jonas knew better than to argue.

Master Percy showed his ticket to a steward and asked where his stateroom was. The man just muttered, "Upper deck," and jerked his head toward a steep, narrow set of steps that was little better than a ladder. Meekly Jonas followed Master Percy through the crowd of people on the lower deck and up to the upper one, where they had more breathing space. There was a row of doors with numbers on them. Master Percy peered at his ticket, then opened a door.

"This is our cabin," he said. "Put my bag on that chair."

"Yes, sir." Jonas set the carpetbag down on the little straight-back chair beside the door. The tiny room had two hard, narrow bunks, one over the other, each made up with starched-looking sheets and a blue blanket. The only other things in it were the chair and a washstand that held a plain white pitcher and bowl.

Master Percy locked the doors on either side of the cabin. Then he sat down on the lower bunk and had Jonas pull off his boots. "I'm going to sleep," he said, stretching out on the bunk. "You stay in here, and keep out of trouble."

"Yes, sir."

Since the carpetbag was on the chair and Jonas didn't dare lie on a bunk, he sat down on the floor. It sure got dreary sitting there, looking at Master Percy's big old stocking feet and listening to him snore. The boat creaked and rattled, and once in a while it wailed like a cow having a calf. That didn't seem like a noise that a good, safe boat ought to make. At last, in spite of the noise, Jonas curled up on the floor and went to sleep. He awoke when something poked him in the ribs.

Master Percy was standing over Jonas, jabbing him with his toe. "Time to eat, boy. And put on your shoes! You can't go to the dining room in your bare feet."

The cabin's rear door opened onto a dining room that was fancier than anything Jonas could have imagined. It ran the whole length of the boat. In the center stood a long row of tables set with lace cloths, candles in silver holders, crystal goblets, gleaming silverware, and gold-rimmed plates. The red carpet was as soft and thick as spring grass. "The Grand Saloon" someone called the room. What a fine name!

The white folks were gathering around the tables. Black waiters filled their water glasses and handed them menus with lots of swirls and curlicues.

After Jonas had gotten Master Percy settled, one of the waiters led him into the kitchen and gave him a tin plate, a dull knife, and a fork that looked as though it had been stepped on. The cook served him a heap of boiled potatoes, a thin slice of pork, and two corn cakes.

The food was good—in tastiness, it was somewhere between Esther's and Mama's cooking—but Jonas got lonesome sitting at the worktable by himself while the waiters and kitchen helpers bustled around, joking and trading gossip. He wished they'd come sit with him, so he could ask them how they liked working on a steamboat and what places they had been to.

After dinner, the tables in the Grand Saloon were pulled apart and arranged in little groups. The ladies gathered at one end of the room and the gentlemen at the other. Master Percy sat down with some men to play cards.

"Begging your pardon, sir," Jonas said. "Will you be needing me?"

"What? No. Go . . ." He waved vaguely. "Go sit in the cabin."

Jonas went back to the cabin, but it was dull and lonely. After a while he went outside to the upper deck and stood at the railing to watch the big, wide Missouri River flow past. It sure was pretty in the twilight, with the dark hills in the background and a thumbnail moon hanging in the sky. How far had they come? What was happening at home? He pictured Leola toting the dishes back to the kitchen, Esther heating the dishwater, Tate playing his flute. Was it only last night that they had been dancing and laughing together?

Suddenly a hand gripped his shoulder and spun him around. It was Master Percy, his face contorted with anger. "How dare you come out here without my permission?"

"I—I didn't think you'd mind, sir."

"Well, you thought wrong." He smacked Jonas across the cheek. "You don't go anywhere without my say-so! You're my family's *property*. Do you understand?"

"Y-yes, sir."

"Don't forget it. Now come help me get ready for bed."

Jonas did as he was told, but his face stung and his

pride stung even worse. Nobody, not even Master Percy, had ever hit him in the face. Nobody had ever called him *property*, either. Of course, he'd always known that the Hoopers owned him, but he thought of himself as a servant, not as an object. Property was a table or a wagon, not a person.

Jonas bit his lip to keep from crying. Esther's words about Master Percy rang in his ears: "No matter what Master Percy do, you try to please him. If you don't, you just be making trouble for your own self."

3

THEY WERE ON THE *MINNEHAHA* FROM SATURDAY UNTIL Monday morning. Both nights Jonas slept on the floor of the stateroom, and both mornings Master Percy woke him up with a poke in the ribs. Both days, Jonas thought he would die of loneliness.

The worst time was Sunday morning, when they stopped at a town called Waverly to unload freight. Master Percy sat on the top deck, smoking his cigar and reading a newspaper, and Jonas stood by the rail near him, listening to the church bells ring and watching people walk to Sunday services. A great pang of homesickness struck his heart as he thought of how the folks at home would be walking to church right now.

Sunday evening was when the widowed doctor was to join them.

Master Percy said, "You're to carry his bags up here

and help him find his stateroom. And look sharp! Don't be lazy or uppity. Understand?"

"Yes, sir." Nobody had ever accused him of being lazy or uppity.

Master Percy cuffed the back of his head. "Don't use that sullen tone of voice!"

"Yes, sir." Jonas tried to sound cheerful. He wanted to rub the sore spot on his head, but he wouldn't let Master Percy know how much it hurt.

As they looked at the crowd of men waiting to board the *Minnehaha*, Jonas tried to pick out Dr. Yoder. He decided the doctor had to be the tall, red-haired man. But as that man walked up the ramp to the boat, a girl in a blue-checked dress followed him. She looked a little younger than Jonas and was plump, with a pale, solemn face. A bit of gingery hair frizzed over her forehead, and the rest was pulled into long braids that looped up like two jump ropes behind her head.

Master Percy had spied the same man. He called out, "Are you Dr. Henry Yoder?"

"Yes, I am!" The doctor came over, a carpetbag in his hands. He didn't look old, but he had a careworn countenance. His red hair was sprinkled with gray, and his gray eyes, which sat close to his arched nose, looked weary.

The two men shook hands, and both said, "Glad to meet you." Then, to Jonas's astonishment, Dr. Yoder put a hand on the little girl's back, drew her forward, and said, "Mr. Hooper, this is my daughter, Sophronia. She'll be coming with us."

Jonas nearly burst out laughing at the look of dismay on Master Percy's face.

"Coming *with* us?" Master Percy shook his head. "I don't mean any disrespect, but nobody said anything about a little gal coming along."

"I hadn't planned it," Dr. Yoder explained, "but an unexpected situation arose. She was going to stay with my brother Edmund and his family, and come out to California to join us when they moved there next fall. But Edmund's wife came down with the dropsy, and . . ." He shrugged. "I have no choice but to bring Sophronia with me. There's been no time to tell Jeremiah Quincy, but I'm sure he'll understand."

"I see," Master Percy finally said. "Well, I suppose it's up to him."

"Indeed," Dr. Yoder said. He held out his boat tickets. "Mr. Hooper, would you be kind enough to show us the way to our cabin?"

"Yes, of course. My boy, Jonas, will carry your bags."

Dr. Yoder gave his carpetbag to Jonas, with a polite nod. When Jonas reached for the girl's little hand trunk, she said, "Thank you, but I can carry it."

"No, miss, please. It be my job to do it." Jonas kept his hand out, waiting.

"Well, all right. I don't want you to get into trouble," she said, giving it to him. The two of them fell into step behind the men. "Are you going to the gold fields, too?"

"Yes, miss."

"Good, I'm glad!" She smiled, and even with his eyes

cast down he could see that smiling perked up her plain face. "I didn't think there'd be anybody else near my age. I'm eleven. I can't wait to see Kansas Territory, can you? I'm sorry about Aunt Prunella's illness, but I'd much rather be here with Papa than with her and Uncle Edmund."

Dr. Yoder looked over his shoulder. "Sophronia, don't wear out Jonas's ears."

"Yes, Papa," she replied.

Jonas liked Miss Sophronia. The next morning, as he was getting Master Percy settled at the breakfast table, he saw her come into the Grand Saloon with her father. She was wearing a blue-and-green-plaid dress with a white pinafore over it, and her braids hung down her back. When she saw Jonas, she gave him a grin and a little wave of her fingers. He wished he could smile or wave back, but all he dared to do was give her a slight nod and lower his eyes respectfully.

Soon after breakfast they reached Kansas City. Master Percy sent Jonas to locate his trunks. Half a dozen deckhands helped to unload them when the boat docked. They must have seen Master Percy and thought he'd pay them well since he was dressed so fine. Jonas knew different, but he was glad they were fooled, because he didn't see how else those trunks would get off the boat unless they sprouted legs and walked.

As Jonas followed Master Percy and the Yoders down the *Minnehaha*'s ramp to the landing, he gazed, awestruck. Such goings-on there were! Five other steamboats were at the landing, all being loaded or unloaded by sweaty, cursing men. Things were piled up everywhere, as high as a house in some places: wooden crates, animal hides, farm plows, bolts of calico, kegs of nails, barrels of whiskey, church bells, and pianos. With all the cattle mooing, donkeys braying, men yelling, and steamboat whistles tooting, Jonas could hardly hear himself think.

Jeremiah Quincy was waiting for them. He was a short, roly-poly, bewhiskered man who had a fierce-looking red face, bright blue eyes, and a fringe of gray hair around the bald dome of his head. He wore a green-plaid flannel shirt and tan woolen pants and held a wide-brimmed felt hat in one hand. In his other hand he held the reins of a stocky black horse.

He and his friend Dr. Yoder greeted each other jovially. Master Percy introduced himself, and Mr. Quincy looked at Jonas. "And what's your name, young man?"

Before Jonas could answer, Master Percy said, "This is my father's servant, Jonas. He'll be doing our cooking and laundry and will help drive the oxen."

Mr. Quincy grinned widely and stuck out his hand. "Pleased to meet you, Jonas. Henry and I sure need help with the cooking, what with me running this train and Henry doctoring everybody."

Jonas hesitated, confused. No white man had ever offered to shake his hand before! What should he do? Finally he reached out and touched his hand to the large white one. Mr. Quincy grasped it and pumped it up and down, the way he'd done with the others. Jonas heard Master Percy sniff in disgust.

Mr. Quincy wasn't any happier than Master Percy had been over Miss Sophronia's coming. He told Dr. Yoder, "Henry, I've made her acquaintance before and I know she's a fine little gal. But we have a long, hard journey ahead, and the gold fields ain't no place for gals. What you ought to do is make arrangements for her to go straight to California with a family. Then as soon as we get out there—"

"I understand, Jeremiah, but I simply won't leave her with folks I don't know."

Mr. Quincy gave a sigh. "All right. I reckon she can come."

While they'd been talking, Miss Sophronia had stood quietly. Now she looked at Mr. Quincy and said, "Thank you, sir. I'm much obliged. And you'll find that I won't be any trouble. I'm very healthy and self-sufficient."

"All right, all right," grumbled Mr. Quincy. "Let's go get outfitted."

When the men weren't looking, Miss Sophronia gave Jonas a big grin.

Outfitted, Jonas discovered, meant buying tools and provisions for the trip. Mr. Quincy had already bought their wagon and oxen. That morning, he had left them near the general store so all the purchases could be loaded quickly.

It turned out that Dr. Yoder had to go to a druggist to

stock up on the medicines he needed to take along. Miss Sophronia said she would go with him.

As Jonas followed Master Percy and Mr. Quincy to the general store, he felt his eyes widen. So this was what a city was like! Shops, saloons, banks, and taverns lined the streets, and the road was crowded with wagons, carts, horses, mules, oxen, and dogs. The sounds of blacksmiths' hammers, carpenters' saws, and tinkling piano music filled the air. It was exciting, but Jonas longed for the quiet of home. Cities, he decided, made his head spin. There was too much noise, and too much to look at.

The store they went to was almost as big as the Hoopers' house. When they got inside, Mr. Quincy said, "Jonas, I'll confess something. All I use for cooking is a rusty skillet and a dented old coffeepot. I don't know what a real cook needs. Can you tell me what sort of tinware we ought to buy?"

"I reckon so, sir."

"What's that?" he bellowed. "Look up and don't mumble, son!"

Timidly, Jonas raised his eyes. "I said, I reckon so, sir."

Master Percy cleared his throat. "I guess you don't have slaves, Mr. Quincy. If you did, you'd know that they're supposed to look down and speak quietly. It shows respect."

"Balderdash!" the older man retorted. "It shows they're being bullied, and it's got no place on the trail."

"But—" Master Percy started.

Mr. Quincy cut him off. "You want somebody to be

looking down at the ground and mumbling *respectfully* when they're saying there's a snake about to nip your backside or an Indian sneaking up behind you with a hatchet? I don't think you do, Mr. Hooper."

Master Percy just scowled the way he did when his daddy scolded him.

Jonas thought that was a good sign. Perhaps Master Percy would be afraid to mistreat him when Mr. Quincy was around.

Master Percy said, "You take Jonas and get the provisions and gear, Mr. Quincy. I'm going to the barber's."

"All right," Mr. Quincy told him. "Meet us back here when you're done."

To Jonas's amazement, Master Percy got out his wallet and handed some money to the older man. "Be obliged if you could get the boy some proper shoes and anything else you think he needs. I don't want people to say I'm not taking care of him."

Mr. Quincy raised an eyebrow. "Of course. I'd be happy to."

Master Percy left, and Jonas followed Mr. Quincy bashfully across the store. What a busy place it was! Clerks scribbled orders, haggled with customers, filled and weighed bags, and collected money. Shop boys climbed ladders and handed down items from shelves. Burly loading men carried goods outside to the waiting wagons.

When Jonas and Mr. Quincy reached the tinware, Jonas felt tongue-tied and miserable. He'd never chosen anything before, and he'd never heard of a white man asking a slave for his opinion. Would he make foolish choices? Would he sound uppity or greedy?

Mr. Quincy said, "Let's start with the most important question. Should we get one of them newfangled cook-stoves, or do you favor cooking over an open fire?"

That was a point on which Mama had had strong feelings.

"Open fire be better, sir," Jonas said. He cleared his throat. "My mama use a cookstove once and she say they got a mind of their own. Problem is, you can't see the flame and tend it yourself—you got to use knobs and numbers. Mama say the only time she ever ruin a roast or turn out dry bread was with that cookstove."

"Well, then, that's that," Mr. Quincy said briskly. "No cookstove for us! Now, what kind of bake kettle is best? And do you like a frying pan with legs, or one without?"

Mr. Quincy was so ignorant about cooking and so grateful for advice that Jonas soon freely answered questions and even offered suggestions. They finished choosing their tinware and went to buy provisions. By that time Jonas felt confident enough to recommend powdered yeast mix, which Mama had preferred to baking powder. When Mr. Quincy asked what kind of flour to buy, he promptly said, "Middlings, sir. Shorts ain't good flour, and superfine be needed only for cake-baking."

"We'd like middlings," Mr. Quincy told the clerk who was measuring out the flour.

The clerk sniggered. "You let a little darky boy tell you what to buy?"

Mr. Quincy looked at him coldly and said, "I let our *cook* tell me what he needs. Now you'd best give us our middlings or I'll take my business elsewhere."

The clerk's eyes grew big and he said, "Yes, sir, middlings it is, sir. A fine choice, sir."

They bought sugar, beans, rice, and cornmeal, and then chose a set of spices. That took a while because Mr. Quincy had to read the labels aloud until they found a set that had all the seasonings Jonas was familiar with. There were still more foodstuffs to buy: bacon, dried fruit, crackers, molasses, salt, tea, coffee, and such. Jonas was starting to think they'd be at the store all night, when finally Mr. Quincy said, "That ought to do 'er!"

While the loading men were carrying everything out to the wagon, Mr. Quincy bought Jonas some flannel shirts and woolen pants to replace his table-waiting clothes, then got him several pair of socks and took him to try on shoes. The ones they selected were sturdy, wide-toed, and so comfortable that Jonas broke out in a big smile when he walked across the floor.

"Thank you, sir." Jonas couldn't stop grinning. "Never knew shoes could be this good-feeling. I sure hope Master Percy give you enough money for all these things."

Mr. Quincy shrugged. "I'll figure it up. If he didn't, I'll just remember to swipe some gold from him when we get to Pikes Peak."

He laughed. Jonas, realizing that he'd been joshing, laughed, too.

By the time the Yoders and Master Percy returned,

the wagon was loaded. They walked alongside it out to McGee's Addition, which Mr. Quincy said was a campground for people who were getting ready to go West. He said they'd stay there for a couple of days, while the other men in the party arrived and prepared for the journey.

So many folks were already camped at McGee's Addition that it was like a town—a canvas town, full of wagons and tents. Many of the wagon covers had words painted on them, and Jonas wondered what they said. He helped Mr. Quincy take the yokes off the oxen, and milked the two cows that made up the middle pair. Mr. Quincy knew how to buy good oxen: all six were handsome, red-hued Devon cattle, like the ones that plowed the fields at home.

Because everyone was tired, supper was just beef jerky, crackers, apples, and fresh milk. Then they chose their sleeping places. Dr. Yoder wanted Miss Sophronia to bed down inside the wagon, but she insisted on sleeping on the ground under the stars. The men would sleep in the small tents; Jonas, under the wagon. After supper Mr. Quincy showed them how to carve out some hollows in the ground to make themselves better sleeping places. Then he taught Master Percy how to put up his tent.

"I don't have to put up any tent," said Master Percy indignantly. "I have a slave boy to do my work. You ought to be teaching *him* how to do it."

Mr. Quincy shook his head firmly. "Mr. Hooper, I always say a man's got to pitch his own tent. Don't matter how many servants he's got. It's just something a man does for himself, like cleaning his own gun."

Master Percy scowled, but Mr. Quincy made him keep working until his tent stood as sturdily as the others. It was the first time Jonas had ever seen anybody make Master Percy work.

Jonas smiled. Mr. Quincy sure was something. What with him and that odd-looking, friendly Yoder gal along, this could be a mighty interesting journey.

4

THE NEXT MORNING JONAS WOKE BEFORE DAWN AND thought, Time to go downstairs and start the kitchen fire. Then, after his head got itself a little more wakeful, he remembered where he was and why.

Mr. Quincy appeared to be the only person up. He had already built a cooking fire, in a shallow pit where the wind wouldn't find it so easily, and he was hunkered down, tending the flame. When he saw Jonas stirring, he stood up and came over.

"Morning, Jonas," he said softly. "It's four-thirty. I was about to wake you up so you can get breakfast going. It don't have to be fancy. Just get the coffee on, then maybe whip up some biscuits and fry some bacon."

"Yes, sir." Sure hope my cooking pleases folks, Jonas thought. At home he'd prepared simple dishes under

Mama's and Esther's supervision, but he'd never fixed a meal on his own. And he knew that even a breakfast of bacon and biscuits could be awful if you measured wrong or let something burn while your mind wandered.

Jonas climbed into the wagon and put on some of the new clothes Mr. Quincy had gotten him. They felt as soft as moss on his skin, and they let him move freely. No more scratchy fabric, tight collars, and binding pant legs! He shoved his old clothes into his flour sack, way down to the bottom where his hurtful old shoes were.

Since Jonas couldn't read the words on the bags and tins, Mr. Quincy helped him find what he needed. To his surprise, the back end of the wagon had a fold-down worktable cleverly built in, which made the biscuit-making a lot easier. He fixed biscuits just the way he remembered Mama making them. Then, on impulse, he decided to stew some dried apples, to round out the meal. He asked Mr. Quincy to get the cinnamon and nutmeg, since he knew Mama had used them in her stewed apples.

It was nice making breakfast with Mr. Quincy, just the two of them working in the cool dawn while the others slept. The birds chirped their morning ditties, and the sky turned from gray to a pale blue-green with pink clouds resting on the horizon. Mr. Quincy ground the coffee and milked the two cows. By the time the sun started up, the bacon was sizzling in the frying pan, the biscuits were browning in the bake kettle, the coffee was bubbling in its pot, the apple mixture was heating in the saucepan, and two pails stood full of fresh, frothy milk. Everything looked good and smelled good. Soon, Jonas thought, they would find out whether it tasted good, as well.

"Roll out! Roll out!" Mr. Quincy yelled to the sleepers, banging on a tin pan with a metal spoon. The din was met with lots of yelling and cussing, some from people in nearby camps.

Jonas couldn't help but laugh. He was surprised at how good that felt, as though a big knot inside him was loosening up.

Breakfast was a roaring success.

After taking his first bite of biscuit, Master Percy looked at Jonas in surprise. "Dang it, boy, where'd you learn to make such good biscuits? These are a sight better than the ones that old Esther woman makes."

"They're delicious!" agreed Dr. Yoder. "Healthy, too. Breadstuffs are good for you."

"These apples are larruping good," Mr. Quincy put in.

It was Miss Sophronia who gave Jonas the best compliment of all. "I think," she said slowly, "that these biscuits just might be as good as the ones Mama used to make."

"Thank you, miss," Jonas said, ducking his head and grinning. He couldn't remember when he'd gotten so many compliments. Feelings of relief, pride, joy, and bashfulness all whirled around inside him, each one trying to shove its way to the top, until he wasn't sure whether he wanted to whoop and holler or go hide his face out of embarrassment. He was glad for dish-washing time, when he could quiet his mind.

Jonas spent the day helping the others repack the wagon. They had to unload everything, check the bags to make sure they were securely sewn closed at the tops, put the sugar into India rubber bags to keep it dry, nail down cleats on the wagon floor to keep things from shifting, and reload exactly as Mr. Quincy told them. "We have to be able to reach the things we'll need on the journey," he said. "Otherwise, we'll end up digging through the whole wagon every evening to find a frying pan or an extra blanket."

It was a lot of work, and most of it fell to Master Percy and Jonas. Dr. Yoder was called away to tend the broken leg of a man in another camp. Miss Sophronia did what she could, but she tired quickly. Mr. Quincy was busy meeting and helping the new members of the train as they arrived.

Master Percy soon got cranky and made Jonas do the bulk of the work.

"You didn't check all those flour bags, you lazy little no-account!" he snapped. "I saw you give them a glance and walk off."

"No, sir, I looked at them up close. Honest, I did," Jonas said. He felt humiliated, having to defend himself to Master Percy.

"Well, check them again. And be careful with my bedroll! If you drop it in the mud, I'll make you sorry."

"Yes, sir," Jonas murmured.

Master Percy swatted him on the ear. "Don't use that sullen tone of voice with me!"

Jonas repeated, "Yes, sir," as cheerfully as he could. He felt like a silly little bird chirping, and he wanted to cry with weariness and vexation.

During the day, Jonas saw five more wagons roll into camp, and counted a-dozen-and-six men: two wagons each carried five men, one wagon carried four, and two smaller wagons each carried two. They all seemed to be young, fit, enthusiastic fellows, eager to get on the trail and certain they'd make their fortunes in the gold fields. From what he overheard, Jonas gathered that he was the only real cook in the train—and the only servant. The other men would all take week-long turns fixing meals for those in their wagons. The four in the two smaller wagons would link up for cooking duties.

When it came time to fix supper, Jonas decided to make potato soup and corn bread. He had helped Mama make potato soup lots of times, and he could have made corn bread in his sleep.

But he had a problem. He needed Mr. Quincy to read the words on the sacks, barrels, and tins so he could find the cornmeal and other ingredients he required. And Mr. Quincy wasn't in camp. When Jonas asked Dr. Yoder where he was, the doctor replied, "Somebody told him that his old partner in the Santa Fe trade was here at McGee's, waiting for his men to gather, so Jeremiah went looking for him. Said he'd be back for supper."

"Thank you, sir," Jonas replied. Who would help him? He felt shy about asking Dr. Yoder, and he certainly was not going to ask Master Percy. Perhaps Miss Sophronia would help! She was so plain, both in her face and in her nature, that it was hard to be bashful around her.

Jonas found her sitting under a tree near the wagon, reading a thick book.

"Hello, Jonas," she said, looking up.

"Begging your pardon, miss, do you reckon you could come read the provision bags for me, so's I can find what I need for supper?"

"I'd be happy to." She put down her book and accompanied him to the wagon.

Once inside, she quickly found the items Jonas asked for. "There you are!" She looked at him curiously. "If you can't read, how do you find things in your kitchen at home?"

Jonas shrugged. "We just keeps everything in the same places all the time: flour in the big bin, cornmeal in the little bin, and so on. The spices, we can sniff at. Esther, our cook, put different marks on the spice canisters she use most."

"Seems like it would be a lot easier if you could read," Miss Sophronia mused. Then, casually, as though it were nothing, she asked, "Would you like me to teach you?"

"Miss?" Jonas couldn't believe his ears. For as long as he could remember, he had wanted to learn to read. Several times he had sneaked a look at Master William's books and wondered how to make sense of those odd marks. Then one day Master William had caught him looking at the cover of a book and had cut his legs with a riding crop until the blood ran down them. Just for looking at the cover! Master had said sternly, "If you ever look at a book again, I'll whip you properly." Then, in a gentler tone, he'd added, "It's for your own good, Jonas. Reading will only teach you rascality and make you impertinent and dissatisfied with your life. Do you understand?" Jonas had said, "Yes, sir," but he hadn't understood. When he'd told Mama about it, she had held him close and cried, "Honey, you leave them books alone! It'd break my heart to see you whipped. Worse, he could sell you and I'd never see you again."

Jonas had promised his mother that he wouldn't look at any more books. But now Mama was gone.

Miss Sophronia was peering at him, waiting for an answer.

Jonas heard himself say, "Yes, miss! Yes, I'd like that more than anything."

As soon as the words were out, he felt both scared and exhilarated.

Miss Sophronia's face lit up. One of her looped braids fell down, but she just brushed it aside. "Oh, good! I'm so glad you want to learn. Back home, my mama had a school for slave children. I used to help her teach them to read."

"And was they able to learn?"

"Why, yes, Mama said they learned faster than white children!" While Jonas was taking that in, she added, "And don't call me Sophronia. I *hate* that name. Call me Sky."

"Sky? You mean, like what's up above?"

"That's right. See, my whole name is Sophronia Kemp Yoder. Kemp was Mama's name before she was married. That makes my initials S.K.Y., and that spells Sky."

"Initials, miss?"

"Yes. Initials are the first letters of your names. You'll understand later. And stop calling me *miss*! I'm just Sky."

Jonas thought a minute. "Begging your pardon, miss, but I reckon I better call you miss. Otherwise, if Master Percy hear me, he'll say I'm being sassy."

Miss Sky snorted. "I hate that Master Percy of yours! I saw him box your ear for no reason."

Jonas was ashamed that she had seen it. He said, "Let's not talk about old Master Percy. I want to know how soon I can start my reading lessons."

"Hmm. Perhaps we can start right now." She looked around and picked up a salt sack. Pointing, she said, "See this first letter? What does it look like?"

"I—I don't know," Jonas replied, bewildered.

"Think! If you saw it slithering along the ground, what would you say it was?"

Jonas blinked at it. In a very low voice, he ventured, "A snake?"

"That's right! The letters tell you what sound to make. This letter's called S, and it tells you to make the *sss* sound, the one you hear in *snake*. It's also at the beginning of the word *salt*, which is what's in this bag. *Ssssnake, ssssalt*. Hear how they sound alike?"

"Yes, miss, I do indeed." Jonas grinned with delight.

"There are twenty-five more letters," Miss Sky told

49

him. "It'll take time to learn them all, but you can go over them in your head while we're walking. And while you're learning new ones, I'll teach you how to make some words with the ones you know."

"Thank you, miss," Jonas said fervently. "I'll work hard."

"Then we have a deal!" She stuck out her hand, and Jonas tentatively touched her fingers. She grabbed his hand and gave it a shake. He knew they were sealing their bargain: she'd teach him and he'd work hard to learn.

"And," she added, lowering her voice, "I won't tell anybody. I'm sure Mr. Quincy wouldn't care, but your Mr. Hooper would be furious."

"What about your daddy?" Jonas asked. "Would he mind?"

Miss Sky was silent for a moment, then slowly replied, "Yes, I'm afraid he would. He thinks that slaves should be taught to read, but only if they have their owners' permission. He doesn't want to cause trouble. He says that much as he hates slavery, he hates violence even more. When Mama opened her school, she had to promise him that she would teach only children who had their masters' approval." Miss Sky smiled, clearly remembering. "Mama put on her best bonnet and went around to talk to the slave owners. She was so sweet and persuasive that nearly all of them let their slave children come."

Something in her voice made Jonas say, "You must miss your mama an awful lot."

"I do. So does Daddy. He hardly ever smiles anymore.

Mama was . . ." Miss Sky shrugged. "Papa says she was the light in our lives. When anything bad happened, she could make it all right with a laugh, or a hug and a kiss. She was always reading books, and she loved to sing. Sometimes after supper she'd read a poem or sing a song to us."

"My mama couldn't read, but she liked to sing," Jonas said. "She sang hymns while she worked. I used to tell her that her pies and jams didn't need no sugar, 'cause they got their sweetness from her singing. And, Lord, could she dance! Sometimes the womenfolk would have a contest to see who could dance the longest with a glass of water on her head. Mama'd always win. She'd never spill a drop. What she loved best, though, was cooking."

"I guess both our mamas loved that." Miss Sky smiled. "You know, I think they would have been friends."

Jonas smiled back shyly. He liked that idea.

A yell came from Master Percy. "Jonas, where are you? We're nigh onto starving!"

"Be right there, sir."

Miss Sky said hastily, "While you're cooking, I'll copy down the alphabet. Later, I'll come help you wash dishes. If the men aren't around, I'll teach you the first few letters."

Jonas was so excited, it was hard to keep his mind on fixing supper. He was going to learn to read! Soon those funny marks on paper would teach him things and tell him stories. A little voice in his head asked, Jonas, what you getting yourself into? How can you be Master

William's manservant when you be hiding that you know how to read? But he told that voice to hush. After all, his manservant days were at least a year off—surely he could figure out something by then. In the meantime, it oughtn't to be too hard to hide it from Master Percy out here on the trail. As Miss Sky had said, he could review his letters while he walked. He could also study at night after everyone was asleep.

While Jonas was stirring the corn bread batter and dreaming about his reading lessons, Mr. Quincy came back into camp. Along with him was what looked like a bear wearing clothes and a slouchy hat.

"Looky here who I found!" Mr. Quincy told everyone gleefully, slapping the bear on his shoulder. "This is Jack Rulo, my old partner in the Santa Fe trade. We used to lead freight wagons down to New Mexico. Jack'll be staying for supper, Jonas, so I hope you've got plenty of vittles."

"Yes, sir," Jonas replied, trying not to stare. He'd never seen anybody as wild-looking as Mr. Rulo. The man's matted black hair, heavy mustache, and bushy beard all blended into one great mass, so that only a little bit of his face showed through. He wore blue jeans-cloth britches; a fringed brown deerskin shirt; soft, beaded deerskin slippers; and that shapeless black hat. Judging from the way he smelled, he was a lot better acquainted with cigars and whiskey than with soap and water.

"Howdy, folks," he said. "Hope you don't mind me

barging in." He grinned at Jonas. "I've been hearing about your cooking. I need a good meal before I hit the trail."

"Yes, sir," Jonas murmured, pleased. He was glad he'd made a large pot of soup.

Supper received as many compliments as breakfast had. As Mr. Rulo started on his third bowl of soup, he said, "Sure wish I had a cook like you, Jonas. I'll be lucky if I can hire anybody half as good."

"Thank you, sir," Jonas replied. Shyly he added, "My mama taught me to cook."

"Did she now?"

Master Percy looked up. "I remember Jonas's mammy. She was a purty thing—slender and well built, with big eyes and real soft-looking skin. She used to wear a red silk dress to church, didn't she, boy?"

"Yes, sir," Jonas muttered. Master Percy had no business talking about Mama in that flirty way! Had he ever pinched Mama on the backside, the way he had Leola? The thought made Jonas want to knock Master Percy down and pummel him. He was grateful when the topic turned to Mr. Rulo's train.

"How many wagons have you got in your train, Jack?" Mr. Quincy asked.

"Twenty-nine," the big bear-man replied. He told them he'd be leading his train to Santa Fe and then southward into the country of Mexico.

"What manner of goods are you hauling?" Dr. Yoder asked.

"Little bit of everything. Calico, sewing needles, shoes, bags of flour, dishes. I'll either sell them or trade them for wool, or goat skins, or some of them fine blankets the Mexicans make. I can sell those in Kansas City when I get back."

The doctor took a swig of coffee. "Which route do you take? The Raton Pass?"

Mr. Rulo reached for another biscuit. "No, sir, I don't like crossing them mountains. Jeremiah'll tell you. There was days when we'd work from sunrise to sunset and barely make half a mile. No, bad as it is, I prefer to cross the Cimarron and go that route. The Jornada del Muerto."

"Jornada—?" repeated Master Percy quizzically.

"—del Muerto," Mr. Rulo finished. "That's Spanish for 'Journey of the Dead Man.'"

"Why is it called that, sir?" Miss Sky asked.

Mr. Rulo explained. "Well, missy, there's a good fifty-mile stretch between the Arkansas and Cimarron rivers where there ain't nothing but sand. No water, no wood, no landmarks, nothing. If you don't start out with a full keg of water, a good supply of food, and a reliable compass, you're as good as dead."

"Helps to have plenty of men and guns along, too," Mr. Quincy added. "The Jornada's where you find the fiercest Indian tribes of all: the Comanche, Kiowa, Apache, and Cheyenne. And then there's the rattlesnakes. How many'd we count last time, Jack?"

"Oh, around fifty or so a day," Mr. Rulo said casually.

Mr. Quincy said, "Then, of course, you got your storms. Hail as big as gold pieces, and wind that'll blow over a loaded wagon. And the lightning! I seen more'n one mule struck dead. Saw a fella struck dead once, too."

Master Percy asked, "Is the money worth that kind of danger?"

"Well, trade's right profitable," drawled Mr. Rulo. "Ain't just that, though. Once you've rode the trail, you don't want a sitting-down life. You want a dash of excitement."

Mr. Quincy snorted. "More like a barrelful of excitement."

"Maybe so," conceded Mr. Rulo, "but, as I recall, Jeremiah, you never complained. Cussed a blue streak, but never complained. Say, young fellow," he added, holding out his tin cup to Jonas, "you suppose I could have some more of that good coffee of yours?"

"Yes, sir," Jonas replied, and went to get the heavy coffeepot that sat beside the fire.

After supper, he started washing the dishes. Dr. Yoder went to bed early, and Master Percy went off to play poker with some fellows at another wagon. Mr. Quincy and Mr. Rulo sat by the fire, drinking whiskey and remembering old times.

Miss Sky had disappeared into the wagon. Jonas was afraid she had forgotten about their deal, but just as he began to wash the dishes, he saw her climb down from the wagon and come hurrying over. Stealthily she pulled a slip of paper out of her pocket and tucked the top of it under the dish-rinsing basin so it wouldn't blow away.

"The alphabet," she whispered. Pairs of marks were lined up neatly down the page. Capital letters and lowercase letters, Miss Sky called them. "They're two ways of making the same letter," she said. "You'll have to learn both."

She picked up a towel. While they washed and dried the dishes, she pointed to each letter, whispered its name, and had Jonas repeat it. He didn't see how he'd ever remember them, but Miss Sky had already thought of that. She had made a second list, of only the first seven letters, and had drawn pictures and written words beside them.

"This is the way Mama used to teach letters," she said. "The pictures help you learn. Look: beside A, there's a picture of a cake and an apple. I wrote each word next to the picture and underlined the *a* in it. Those are the two sounds the letter *a* makes."

Jonas nodded, beginning to understand. "Like the *s* making the sound in *snake*!"

"Exactly! I declare, you're going to be my best student," she said, and they laughed.

While they finished the dishes, they went over the rest of the short list. Jonas put both lists in his pocket. Later, when he was in his bedroll, he carefully pulled them out again. There was only a first-quarter moon in the sky, but he could see well enough to make out the characters. So this is reading, he thought, smiling. He traced over the letters with his finger and mouthed the names of the items in the pictures. He kept at it for a long time. When he finally went to sleep, the list was safely back in his pocket, and the alphabet letters danced and sparkled in his dreams.

5

SEVERAL TIMES DURING THE NIGHT, JONAS WOKE UP TO hear Mr. Quincy and Mr. Rulo talking and laughing in low voices. The next morning both men came to breakfast looking haggard and hungover. Jonas had made bacon and fried potatoes, and he tried not to stare when Mr. Rulo ate them off the tip of his knife.

"These vittles sure is lip-smacking good," he told Jonas. "If we's to meet up ahead somewheres, I hope you won't mind me joining you for some more meals."

"No, sir, I won't mind," Jonas replied bashfully. He'd never met anybody like Mr. Rulo before. The man was bigger than life, more colorful than trees in the fall.

As he watched their guest ride off, Mr. Quincy came up to stand with Jonas. He said, "I'll tell you something, Jonas. That there's the biggest-hearted man in the world. He ain't real decorative and his ways could use some polish, but he's honest and dependable. You can always count on him." Then he gave a great sigh and said, "Well, we better get ready to hit the trail."

Everyone spent the morning making final preparations for the trip. To Master Percy, "final preparations" seemed to mean giving Jonas orders. Jonas held a mirror and water bowl while the master shaved; fetched his camp stool and letter-writing kit from the wagon; fanned the flies away while he wrote letters; cleaned his boots; spread out his bedroll and pillow to air; and fixed him lemonade out of water, citric acid, and lemon flavoring.

As usual, Master Percy was quick to humiliate and to slap. When Jonas handed him what he thought was a cigar case, the master smacked him on the jaw and cried, "This is a tobacco box, you nincompoop! Were you put on Earth just to vex me? Bring me my cigar case, and be quick about it!" Jonas ran back to the wagon and searched frantically until he found the small silver container of cigars. But when he presented it to Master Percy, the master airily said, "Take it away, boy! I've changed my mind."

After a lunch of crackers, dried fruit, and beef jerky, the men yoked up the oxen and Mr. Quincy cried, "Let's head West!"

Someone shouted, "Ho for Pikes Peak!"

Miss Sky hollered, "Hoorah!" and tossed her sunbonnet into the air, which brought a chuckle from her father.

The oxen began plodding forward, the big wagon wheels started turning, and the Quincy train slowly pulled out of camp. Mr. Quincy's wagon was in the lead. He drove the oxen, walking beside them with goads. Master Percy and Dr. Yoder walked alongside the wagon, and Jonas trailed them by a few paces. Miss Sky darted here and there, studying whatever caught her eye: a clump of wildflowers, a graceful cottonwood tree, a bright-winged butterfly, or the stone wall of a farm.

Soon they left Missouri and crossed into Kansas Territory. Tall grass with little tasseled ends rippled all around them, and groves of cottonwood trees showed where the creeks were. The wildflowers were a sight to behold! Jonas reckoned that every kind of flower God made must be blooming in Kansas Territory. There were sweet little white ones, round yellow sunshiny ones, tall pink feathery ones, delicate purple ones, and red ones as bright and bold as fire.

Over the following days, he learned that Kansas Territory, like Missouri, got more than its share of springtime rain. At home, a heavy rain just meant putting buckets under the leaks in the kitchen roof. Out here, it meant sitting in camp all morning waiting for the rain to end, then slogging through mud as thick as cake batter. Men slipped in the mud, oxen's hooves got sucked down into it, and wagons got mired so deep that everyone had to push and shove to get them out. Master Percy grew short-tempered.

One morning he snapped, "What kind of cook are you, giving us crackers and dried fruit to munch on? We're *hungry*, boy!"

"Can't make a fire in the rain, sir," Jonas replied. "Even Mr. Quincy tried."

"Well, dang it, boy, you know it's apt to rain in the mornings, so why don't you make breakfast the night before? Even cold beans and biscuits would be better than these durned crackers. You could stew some of this fruit, too, the way you did those apples."

"Yes, sir. I'll try, sir."

That night, he stayed up after the others had gone to sleep so he could prepare food for the next day. In the morning it was drizzling, but he was able to start a large enough fire to reheat a small pot of beans with the bacon spread on top. He held an umbrella over the pot as he stirred it.

Everyone was delighted.

"Look, Jonas has a hot breakfast ready!" Miss Sky exclaimed.

"That'll take the chill off us," her father added, giving Jonas one of his rare smiles.

"Sure is nice having beans and bacon on a rainy morning," Mr. Quincy said, piling his plate high. "Thank you, Jonas. You must have stayed up half the night, cooking."

"It was my idea," Master Percy put in quickly.

"I'm sure it was," Mr. Quincy shot back. "But Jonas is the one who did the work."

"And he's the only cook in camp who did," Miss Sky said smugly. "The men in the other wagons are having to eat crackers."

Jonas smiled, glad that he had pleased them. Over the next few days, he found that even on sunny mornings it was good to have some food already prepared for noon meals and quick suppers. For once Master Percy had had a good idea.

But how Jonas hated staying up late to cook! Not only did his body long for bed, but, worse, his mind wrestled with the terrors of the nighttime prairie. Far-off hills loomed like crouching beasts, and lone sycamore trees waved their arms in the wind, like devils beckoning. Even tall wildflowers that delighted his eyes in the daytime looked evil when they stood black and swaying in the pale moonlight. Coyotes yipped and owls hooted, sounding like lost souls. Jonas felt small and lonely and thought longingly of his cozy attic back home.

It was a relief when one day Mr. Quincy called the whole train together and announced, "Tomorrow night we'll start setting guards. There'll be one pair from darkness to midnight, and another pair from midnight to dawn. The second pair will wake up that week's cooks to start breakfast. I'll make a roster and pass it around."

"You worried about Indians?" a small, sandy-haired man asked nervously.

Mr. Quincy replied, "I ain't scared they'll scalp us, if that's what you mean. Most of the Indians in these parts are Kaws, and they want food, not scalps. I don't mind sharing, but I don't want them taking everything we have. I also don't want our oxen getting loose and wandering off so's we have to hunt for them in the mornings."

That night, as the biscuits baked, the apples stewed, and the men snored, Jonas sat down on the ground and pulled out his alphabet list. He used a stick to write A and

B in the dirt. After he had written each one several times, he rubbed them out and tried writing them without looking at the piece of paper. He made an *A*, but then he had to pause and think about which way the *B* should face.

Suddenly a movement caught his eye. He whirled around.

"It's all right, son," came Mr. Quincy's voice. He grinned. "Looks like Miss Sophronia's got herself a new student."

"Yes, sir." Jonas was shaking all over, and his heart was about to pound its way right through his skin. "I—I didn't know anybody was awake."

"Only me, and only because I have to make that dang guard roster. I was in the wagon, hunting a pen and some paper. I didn't mean to scare you. If I'd seen what you were doing in time, I would have made a racket so you'd know somebody was coming." Mr. Quincy sat down beside him. "Mind if I share the campfire? Here, let me show you how to hold a pen and write on paper."

"Thank you, sir!"

With some guidance from Mr. Quincy, Jonas learned to write *A*, *B*, and *C* without looking at the list. He couldn't keep a smile off his face—with those three letters and *S*, he knew four letters already!

"You're a quick learner," Mr. Quincy said. "Won't be long till you're reading big old books like Miss Sophronia."

Jonas laughed as he pictured himself poring over a hefty book.

Mr. Quincy chuckled, too. Then his face got serious

and he laid his pen down on the roster. "How's your master going to feel about your reading? I don't mean that fool you're traveling with; I know you have to hide it from him. I mean the man you call Master back home."

"Master William, you mean. I'll have to keep it a secret from him, sir. Ain't sure how I'll do it." Jonas thought a moment and said, "Mr. Quincy, there's something I don't rightly understand. Master William told me once that learning to read would teach me rascality and make me impertinent and dissatisfied with my life. Can you figure out why he said that?"

Mr. Quincy gave a laugh, but he didn't sound amused. "Likely he's scared you'll read things he doesn't want you reading."

"You mean like his private letters and such?"

"No, I mean like antislavery pamphlets that would make you decide to rebel, and maps that would help you escape. Besides, once you know how to write, you can forge yourself passes to leave your master's property."

Jonas shook his head, confused. "But why would he think I'd do them things?"

"Because he knows you're smart," Mr. Quincy said promptly. "And there's nothing that scares most slave-owning men more than a smart slave." He gave a long sigh. "Son, your Master William may not put shackles on your feet, but as long as he keeps you ignorant, he's got shackles on your mind, and they're every bit as binding."

Jonas didn't reply. He thought he agreed with Mr.

Quincy, but it made him feel disloyal to Master William—and that was a new and uncomfortable feeling.

"We'll talk about it again one of these days," Mr. Quincy said. "Right now, though, young scholar, you better rescue those biscuits and apples from burning, and then go get some sleep."

The next morning was hot, bright, and dry. Jonas wanted to run around and look at the flowers, the way Miss Sky was doing, but the first time he strayed off the path, Master Percy grabbed him by the arm and hauled him back.

"You stay right behind me, you hear?" he said, giving Jonas's arm a painful jerk.

After that, Jonas obediently stayed in his place, a few paces behind Master Percy. But even though Master Percy could tell his feet where to walk, nobody could tell his head what to think. While he walked, he thought *A*, *B*, *C*, and as soon as he had a chance to peek at his alphabet list, he learned *D* and *E*. He still didn't understand just how letters went together to make words, but when he looked around he thought about how things might be spelled. The word *trees*, for instance, had to have *e*'s in it. And when he whispered *grass*, he could hear that hissing letter that started the word *snake*.

As he was walking, he thought about other things, too. Questions came into his mind that had never bothered him until now. He was grateful that Miss Sky was so friendly and knowledgeable.

One day, while the two of them were picking goose-berries over the midday break, Jonas asked, "Miss Sky, if we was to keep walking for the rest of our lives, where'd we end up?"

She looked at him, her small face shaded by her calico sunbonnet. "We'd end up back where we started, because the earth is round, like a ball."

"Like a *ball*?" Jonas sat back on the ground, a plucked gooseberry still in his fingers, and stared at her. "You fooling me, miss?"

She shook her head solemnly. "No, not one bit. We couldn't walk all the way around it, though, because we'd have to cross the oceans."

She saw his blank look and explained about oceans. She said they were like the biggest lakes he could imagine—each one was thousands of miles across, and deeper than anybody knew. "If we kept walking and walking, we'd get to one. We'd have to cross it in a boat about a hundred times the size of the *Minnehaha*. When we reached shore, we'd be in a foreign land. We'd have to walk a long ways, then take another boat across another ocean to get back to America."

Jonas shook his head, trying to take it all in. "I didn't know the earth was like a ball or that there was all that water."

Miss Sky said, "I brought my geography book, and it has pictures and maps in it. I'll show it to you sometime."

"Thank you, miss." Jonas smiled. He knew that maps

showed you how to get from one place to another, but he couldn't imagine how they did it.

When the Quincy party got back on the trail the next morning, Mr. Quincy asked Jonas to drive the lead wagon. "Let's see how you do," he said, handing Jonas the ox goad. "Think you can handle it?"

"Yes, sir." Jonas was nervous. What if the oxen wouldn't obey him, or he lost the trail? He'd driven oxen only a few times, just up and down the field, plowing furrows.

But with some help from Mr. Quincy, he got the six oxen to move out. Soon it was fun walking beside them, guiding them with the goad and with his voice. Leading the train made him felt important, like Moses leading his people to the Promised Land. Besides, while he was driving the oxen, he didn't have to chase bees away from Master Percy or stop to pull off the master's boots and dump pebbles out of them.

During the day, Jonas saw long trains of huge freight wagons that Mr. Quincy said were headed for Santa Fe. After the first few trains, he started counting them. He got up to a-dozen-and-four trains heading toward Santa Fe, and a-dozen-and-six making the return trip back to Kansas City. He hoped one of the Santa Fe–bound trains might be Mr. Rulo's, and that the big bear-man would come to supper again. But most of the drivers were small dark men who yelled at their mules in a language he didn't understand. None of them looked at all like Mr. Rulo.

Another long walk the next day brought the Quincy

train close to a town called Council Grove. They stopped at a campground like the first one: a temporary city of canvas-covered wagons. Mr. Quincy called the men together and said, "We'll be staying here for a couple of days to cut timber and lay in some extra wagon parts."

Master Percy frowned. "We're not making very good time. At this rate, there won't be any gold left when we get to Pikes Peak."

"If we don't have some spare wagon parts, we may not get there at all," Mr. Quincy shot back. "After we leave here, the trees will get scarce. If a wagon breaks down, we'll have to have the parts we need." He looked Master Percy in the eye. "Once we get farther west, you'll see the sun-bleached bones of fellows who were just like you—in too much of a hurry to prepare for the crossing."

Master Percy swallowed hard and muttered, "I reckon we can spare a day or two."

Some of the other men laughed.

"I reckon we better," Mr. Quincy said dryly. He added, "Anybody who ain't able to chop wood will be given other chores, such as mending or laundry. Wagon leaders, you can task your men as you see fit."

He assigned Jonas and Miss Sky to do laundry. All the clothes Master Percy dumped into Jonas's arms were so stiff with mud that they probably could have walked down to the river on their own.

"These things better be clean when you bring them back," the master said, "even if it takes you the whole day to scrub them. Understand?"

"Yes, sir," Jonas replied. He didn't care how long it took. He knew that while he and Miss Sky worked, she would be helping him with his reading.

Along with a few men from the other wagons, Jonas and Miss Sky carried bags of washing down to the Neosho River, which ran close to camp. They chose a site a little away from the men, and as the two of them soaked, rubbed, and pounded the muddy clothes, they reviewed Jonas's letters. He knew up to *F* now, and Miss Sky skipped ahead and taught him *J*, the letter his name began with. When she drew it in the mud with a stick, he liked the way it stood up so tall and graceful, with that fishhook curve at the bottom. My *J* be a proud letter, he thought.

Miss Sky also taught him his numbers past twelve. They were easy to figure out once he understood the pattern.

After a while, Jonas had to grin at the picture of Miss Sky standing there with her bare feet in the water, the hem of her skirt soaking wet, ginger frizzes of hair sticking out from under her huge sunbonnet, and her blue eyes round and serious as she talked about letters and numbers. She didn't look at all the way he'd pictured a schoolmarm. She was a good teacher, though, and he told her so.

"Hope you aim to be a schoolmarm, miss," he said. "You'd be a fine one."

"Why, thank you, Jonas!" she replied, giving him one of her big smiles. "I do hope to be one someday." As she scraped a stubborn bit of mud off her daddy's pants, she said, "I hope you're going to be a cook when you grow up."

He shook his head. "No, miss. Master William want me to be his manservant. Soon as I get home, he be sending me to get trained by his daddy's manservant, Ebenezer. And that old Ebenezer, he be the best manservant in the world."

"You're going to be a manservant?" Miss Sky's light-colored eyebrows went up in surprise. "Is that what you want to be?"

Automatically, he answered, "Why, yes, miss." But the idea wasn't nearly as appealing as it had been back home. He'd have to hide not only his reading but his curiosity and his new hunger for more knowledge. He wasn't sure he could do that.

As he scrubbed Master Percy's plaid shirt, he thought hard. He had been away from home only two weeks. But when he'd left Split Oak Farm, he'd been an ignorant little servant boy. Now he knew eight letters of the alphabet, and soon he'd be able to read. He was learning to count beyond a dozen. He could make meals that had men cleaning their plates and asking for more. He could lead a wagon train. He'd ridden on a steamboat, seen a city, and shopped for goods in a store. He knew two white people who treated him as an equal. Most important of all, he knew that his head was as good as anybody else's—and that Master William didn't want him knowing that.

The problem was, how would the new Jonas fit into the old Jonas's life?

6

To Jonas's delight, Mr. Rulo showed up for supper.

"Why, I thought you'd be way ahead of us by now!" Mr. Quincy cried, slapping him on the back.

"Aw, I was, but we had a run of bad luck," replied Mr. Rulo. "A wagon wheel came off, then an axle busted and two mules got sick. We've been hunkered down in the same spot for three days. I figured you might be catching up with us, so I rode back a little ways to see if I could find you."

He saw Jonas and waved. "Came back for some more of your fine cooking!" he proclaimed, his grin just visible through the black whiskers. "Reckon it'll be the last good meal I'll have for many a week. I hired on a couple of teamsters who say they can cook, but I don't know as I believe them. So far they ain't served me nothing but mush."

In honor of their guest, Jonas sliced the bacon extra

thick. He added molasses to the boiled beans and baked them, picked and stewed some fresh greens, and whipped up an extra batch of biscuits. He stewed some gooseberries and dropped in dumplings made out of sweetened biscuit dough.

As he cooked, the wind ripping across the high bluffs blew smoke into his face, and no matter how quickly he moved around the campfire, it seemed to move with him. Still, the watering eyes and burning throat turned out to be worthwhile.

"This is purely delicious," Mr. Rulo said as he ate his gooseberry dumplings.

"I think you outdid yourself, Jonas," Mr. Quincy added. "There any more?"

"Yes, sir." Pleased, Jonas put down his plate and went to get the pan with the dumplings, which was keeping warm beside the fire.

When they finished, not a single gooseberry or crumb of dumpling was left.

The Quincy party sat up late, listening to Mr. Quincy and Mr. Rulo spin tales about their days together on the Santa Fe Trail. The men from the other wagons in the train came over to listen, as well. Jonas was fascinated by the talk of lost caravans, Indian attacks, and desperate searches for water. But his favorite parts were the descriptions of that land to the south, where Mr. Rulo said he'd go to finish trading when he left Santa Fe. Jonas whispered the name, *Mexico*, savoring its strangeness. Mr. Quincy and Mr. Rulo used other names that were unlike any he'd ever heard: there were rivers called Rio Grande and Pecos, mountains called Sangre de Cristo, towns named Las Vegas and Albuquerque, a Mexican state named Chihuahua, a trail called Camino Real.

And the way people lived in Mexico! When the two old travelers described it, Jonas could hardly believe his ears. In Mexico, the houses were made of sun-baked mud bricks and had open spaces, called patios, right in the middle of them. Wealthy people decorated their homes with mirrors and ate from silver plates. People cooked their meat inside dried corn husks and ate peppers so spicy that their noses and mouths burned. Men made sport out of fighting bulls, and they danced with dark-eyed beauties at dances called *fandangos*.

It sounded as fanciful and make-believe as the gold fields once had. Jonas thought of how astonished Esther, Leola, and Tate would be when he told them about Mexico.

Jonas rested his head on his knees, taking in the men's words as they washed over him. From far off, he could hear Indians whooping and wolves howling, but he wasn't scared, what with two guards posted and Mr. Rulo and Mr. Quincy there.

Finally Mr. Quincy yawned. He said, "Reckon we better get us some sleep," and went to find their visitor a spare bedroll.

In the morning Jonas fixed a big breakfast of flapjacks and molasses. After they had eaten, Mr. Rulo saddled his buckskin horse and prepared to leave.

"Will you be staying in the area for another day or two?" Dr. Yoder asked him.

The big man shook his head. "No, if the mules have recovered, we'll be leaving today."

"I hope we'll see you again, sir," said Miss Sky.

"Why, thank you, little lady! I hope so, too. We'll be following the same trail for a while yet. Then I'll cross the Arkansas River and head south—"

"To the Jornada del Muerto," Miss Sky put in.

Mr. Rulo smiled. "That's right. And you folks will follow the river for a spell, then swing northwest up to Pikes Peak."

He shook everyone's hand and wished them luck in the gold fields.

"Jonas, take care of yourself," he said.

"Thank you, sir," Jonas replied, thinking how small his hand felt in that big bear paw. He suddenly wished he was going with Mr. Rulo, riding off to that strange land of hot peppers, silver plates, and *fandangos*.

Master Percy gave him a clout on the shoulder. "Quit daydreaming, boy! You've got work to do."

Later that morning the Quincy train crossed the river and went into Council Grove. It was smaller than Kansas City. Its one street was packed with people, wagons, oxen, horses, mules, and dogs, and was thick with dust. Indians who Mr. Quincy said were from the local Kaw tribe lounged against the buildings and came up to beg. Mr. Quincy knew some of them and stopped to converse.

Jonas was scared and fascinated at the same time. He

had never imagined that people could look so different from the folks at home! The Kaws' skin was coppery, and they had narrow strips of hair that stood up like roosters' combs. They wore red or blue cloths around their waists and soft tan leggings. Some wore plaid flannel shirts, much like his own. Others were bare-chested and wore huge necklaces made of buttons, or what appeared to be animals' claws, strung together.

After Mr. Quincy had talked with some of the Kaw men, he grumbled, "Makes me mad as a hornet to see what they've been reduced to. The Kaws used to be a proud tribe, and now they're having to beg. The dang white men have stolen all their land—tricked them into signing phony papers."

Jonas felt sorry for them. Still, he was frightened enough to hang behind Master Percy whenever any of them came close.

Mr. Quincy took the Yoders, Master Percy and Jonas, and some men from the other wagons to a store called the Last Chance. "The name ain't a lie," he said. "The next store you'll see will be in the gold fields."

Jonas was trying not to stare at the signs in the store's windows, but he saw letters that he was certain were *B*'s, *E*'s, *A*'s, and *S*'s. If only he could get a few minutes alone, he could match up the other letters with the ones on his alphabet list and perhaps figure out some words. His desire to do so was even stronger than his fear of the Indians.

" 'Scuse me, sir," he said to Master Percy. "If you won't be needing me, I could just wait outside here."

To Jonas's disappointment, the master shook his head firmly. "Oh, no, boy! I'm not leaving you out here to laze around in the sunshine. You can dang well come in and wait on me, like you're supposed to. You can wipe that sullen look off your face, too, unless you want a good smack across it."

"Yes, sir," Jonas muttered.

Master Percy made a few small purchases. As he was paying for them, Dr. Yoder came up and spoke to him, calling him by name. The long-bearded clerk behind the counter looked up quickly.

"Your name Hooper?" he asked. When Master Percy nodded, he continued, "There was a couple of fellows in here just this morning asking if a Hooper from near Boonville, Missouri, had come through."

"I'm from near Boonville," Master Percy said eagerly. "What did they look like?"

"Oh, they was both dark-haired boys. One was tall and skinny and had a billy-goat beard on his chin. The other was shorter and heftier. He had a walleye, as I recollect."

Master Percy slapped his thigh with glee. "Dag and Bud Chalmers! Well, if that doesn't beat all! I figured they were behind us somewhere. They weren't planning to leave until a few days after we did."

The clerk was rummaging under the counter. "They left a note for me to pass along if you came through. Let's see—here it is."

He handed over a slip of paper and then began ringing up Dr. Yoder's purchases.

"Any news?" the doctor asked Master Percy, who was eagerly reading the note.

"They say they're traveling light and by themselves. Driving mules, too. No wonder they're making such good time." He read further, and grinned. "They're aiming to stay in town this afternoon. Why, I bet I can find them! Wouldn't that be something if we caught up with Dag and Bud? Maybe they'd join up with us. We'd have some high times then, wouldn't we, boy?"

He nudged Jonas hard with his elbow.

"Yes, sir," Jonas replied. He didn't want Dag and Bud Chalmers to join Mr. Quincy's wagon train. He had never met them because Master William had threatened to shoot them if they ever came calling, but he had heard their names plenty of times. Master William and Miz Julia claimed they were the ones who had introduced Master Percy to drinking, gambling, and carousing. The two brothers got into brawls, and they'd been thrown into jail more than once. Even as boys, they'd been troublemakers: they had burned down schoolhouses, thrown rocks through church windows, overturned gravestones, and even poisoned people's dogs, all just for devilment.

Jonas trotted behind Master Percy all over town, looking for the Chalmers boys. He prayed, Lord, don't let us find them. His prayer seemed to be answered. A few people remembered seeing a couple of men fitting Dag and Bud's description, but that was all.

Finally Mr. Quincy came after Jonas and Master Percy

and said, "I'm sorry, Mr. Hooper, but we have to get on the trail. I want to make Diamond Spring by sunset."

Master Percy pouted like a little boy, but Jonas smiled as he drove the lead oxen out of town and back onto the trail.

The sun was setting when the Quincy train reached camp. Diamond Spring was worth the long walk. It was beautiful, with a big, clear spring of icy cold water bubbling up from a rock that was surrounded by mint. Jonas drank his fill and breathed in the sweet, refreshing air.

Mr. Quincy had him pick some mint and taught him how to make a drink called mint julep for the men. Then, since it was so late, Jonas fixed a simple meal of bread and butter, stewed apples, and tea. Afterward Dr. Yoder got out his fiddle. As the men from the other wagons gathered around, he played all manner of songs: toe-tapping ones, foolery ones, and grieving ones. Miss Sky was persuaded to sing, and her voice rose clear and sweet in the night air, reminding Jonas of Tate's flute.

Then, suddenly, the tender duet of voice and fiddle was interrupted by a raucous yell.

"Whoo-ha! If it ain't Percy Hooper in the flesh!"

Master Percy whooped. "Why, if it ain't Dag and Bud Chalmers!" He leaped up, and the three men exchanged back slaps and boisterous handshakes. Jonas tried not to scowl. The Chalmers brothers looked as unsavory as the rats that occasionally scuttled out from under the storage buildings at home. They both had long, greasy brown hair and wore dirty, rumpled clothes. The taller one, Dag, had a scraggly beard. His brother had dark stubble on his cheeks and one eye that turned outward instead of looking straight ahead.

Master Percy introduced his friends to Mr. Quincy and Dr. Yoder. Everyone shook hands and said, "Pleased to meet you," but all four men looked wary and distrustful rather than pleased. Dr. Yoder quietly excused himself, and he and Miss Sky slipped off to the wagon. The rest of the men drifted away.

Master Percy didn't seem to realize that he'd broken up the party, or else he didn't care. "Sit down by the fire and make yourselves at home," he told his friends happily. He turned to Jonas. "Fix some of those mint juleps for my friends."

"Ain't got no more mint, sir," Jonas replied.

"Then go pick some, you fool!" Master Percy cried, clapping his hands under Jonas's nose as though he were shooing off birds. "Make it quick!"

Mr. Quincy cleared his throat. "It's awful dark to be walking down to the spring, Mr. Hooper. We best be getting to bed, anyways. The first guard will be coming on soon." He stood up. "Perhaps your friends wouldn't object to having a quiet drink of whiskey and then showing themselves back to their camp."

"You throwing us out, old man?" Dag Chalmers cried angrily.

Jonas saw Mr. Quincy's eyes narrow. "Ain't throwing

nobody out, son. Just asking a favor of some fellow travelers. We got a long walk tomorrow, and I reckon you do, too."

"You didn't worry about losing sleep when your friend Rulo was here," Master Percy complained. "How come my friends don't get the same kind of welcome?"

Mr. Quincy just said, "Good night, boys," and calmly walked off to his tent.

"Gol-durned man thinks he's my pa," Master Percy grumbled. "Make yourselves at home, fellows, and don't worry about the old man. Jonas, I thought I told you to go pick some mint and make us drinks. Are you going or not?"

Jonas said hesitantly, "Mr. Quincy be right, sir. Ain't safe, going down by the water in the dark, what with them slippery rocks and all."

"Oh, all right." Master Percy waved an impatient hand. "Bring us some whiskey."

"Yes, sir."

Jonas started to walk to the wagon, but Dag Chalmers grabbed him by a handful of hair and tugged his head back, nearly breaking his neck. "I thought your master told you to fix us mint juleps."

"Careful, Dag!" Master Percy said sharply. "The boy's my father's. I don't want him damaged."

"Aw, I ain't hurting him. So, what about it, boy? Your master gave you an order. Have you gone deaf?"

"No, sir." Jonas could tell from the man's breath that he'd already had plenty of drink for one evening.

"Then you're getting mighty sassy, boy. Maybe we ought to whup you. Percy, don't you make this boy mind you?"

"Aw, Dag, sure I do. But if he slips on those rocks and kills himself, my papa'll have my hide."

Bud Chalmers guffawed. "Your papa'll have your hide for bringing home an uppity slave boy, too! I reckon he's had his fill of them."

"That's right." Dag gave Jonas's hair a final cruel tug and let it go. "You better watch your step, or you'll wind up dead like that boy that ran off from your master's place right after you left."

Jonas's heart pounded. Without thinking, he turned and raised his eyes. "What boy?"

Dag slapped him. "Don't you be looking me in the eye!"

All Master Percy said was, "Jonas, quit causing trouble and go get the whiskey."

"But, sir—"

"Get the whiskey, or I'll take a whip to you!"

Jonas picked up a lantern and started for the wagon. With his free hand, he rubbed his throbbing cheek. He was shaking with fear and dread. *Dead like that boy that ran off* . . . Who had run off?

"Go on, sit down," he heard Master Percy say to his friends. "Tell me about the doings at home. You say one of Papa's folks ran off?"

Jonas leaned against the back of the wagon, holding his breath so he could hear.

"Couple of them did, plus several of your grandpa's," came Bud's voice. "Guess it happened just—oh, a day or so after you left."

His brother continued. "Bud and I were in the posse that went after them."

"Papa let you two ride in his posse?" Master Percy cried in astonishment.

"Yeah." Dag chuckled. "He made it clear he wasn't too fond of us, but since we'd volunteered he could hardly say no. Anyways, we found the slaves in a cave down by the river. There were six of them: a young boy and gal from your pa's place and three men and a woman from your grandpa's. We caught them, tied them up in your grandpa's barn, and left Bud to guard them."

Bud put in bitterly, "They made me do it 'cause I was the youngest one in the posse. Almost got me killed, too. They was in the house and—"

"*I'm* telling this story!" Dag snapped. "The rest of us was inside the house having a drink of your grandpa's good whiskey when Bud came in screaming that that mean little black-skinned man they called Richard had got loose. Durned if he hadn't snuck up on Bud and grabbed his gun!"

Dag and Master Percy whooped with laughter.

Bud cried, "It weren't my fault! I was plumb tuckered out and fell asleep."

"Anyways," Dag continued, "Bud woke up just as Richard and your pa's boy were both heading out the barn door. They didn't get far, though. We caught them down by your grandpa's pond. Richard shot at us a couple of times. Then he must have lost his nerve, because he threw the gun to that boy and took off running."

There were more whoops of laughter. Jonas felt himself trembling. He knew what happened to slaves who had a gun in their hands—even if they didn't plan to use it.

Dag said, "That boy was so scared, his eyes was like saucers! Of course your pa shot him down. Otherwise, the kid might have come to his senses and started shooting at us."

Sweet Jesus, thought Jonas. Master William killed Tate.

"Your pa caught up with Richard and killed him, too," Bud added. "He said that's the only thing you can do with a slave that steals guns."

"All the others got whipped and sold South," Dag added. "You never heard such shrieking and howling! The little gal kept yelling that the dead boy was her brother, and that she'd just followed the runaways to talk him into coming home. Your pa ain't stupid. He said, 'You're not fooling me for a minute, you sorry wench,' and left her to be whipped and sold with the others."

Leola! Jonas gasped. He sank to the ground and buried his head in his hands.

Bud chortled. "The slave buyer came around the very next day and hauled them off. Reckon they're enjoying the warm sunshine down in the cotton fields by now."

Master Percy said, "Well, I'm kind of sorry to hear it. That must have been Papa and Mama's housegal, and she was a right purty thing. Still, I'm glad they got caught. If you ask me, there've been too many escapes around there lately. It's time somebody put a stop to them."

"You'll never guess who put a stop to this one," Dag said. "You know that old manservant of your grandpa's who looks like he's about a hundred years old?"

Master Percy snickered. "You mean that old codger Ebenezer?"

"Yeah, that's his name. Well, one of the darkies had a lady friend who worked in the house, and old Ebenezer heard him telling her about how he was going to escape. Ebenezer ran and told your grandpa. They were just waiting for those slaves to run off so they could take a posse to the cave and catch the whole bunch."

Bud said, "Your grandpa called Ebenezer a hero and gave him a bag of money. The old darky was so proud, he nearly popped his vest buttons."

They all laughed at the picture.

"Hey, where's that whiskey?" Master Percy cried. "Where'd that boy get to?"

Jonas got the bottle and took it to him. He was amazed at how his body went on doing what it had to do—handing Master Percy the whiskey bottle, saying, "Good night, sir," getting out his bedroll, and crawling under the cover—while his mind was numb with grief.

The men sat around the campfire, drinking and talking, until all hours. Lying in his bedroll, Jonas heard them, but he didn't pay them any mind. The words tramped through his brain over and over: Tate was shot dead. Leola got whipped and sold South. Ebenezer turned in the runaways—the same Ebenezer that's going to train me. The same Ebenezer I always wanted to be like.

7

THAT NIGHT, JONAS HAD TERRIBLE DREAMS: GUNSHOTS rang out, whips cracked, and people bled and fell and screamed. In between the dreams, he awoke, feeling weak and chilled.

Tate, he thought, must have known he was going to escape, that night at the party. He must have been putting on an act so that nobody, not even his sister or his best friend, would suspect anything. Had he been scared they'd go running to Master William?

Maybe, Jonas thought bitterly, it was easy for house servants to act the way Ebenezer did after a while. They got to thinking so hard about how to please the master that they forgot everything else.

Finally he drifted back into an uneasy sleep.

In the morning, he dragged himself out of his bedroll. He milked the cows, made coffee, fried bacon, baked biscuits, reheated a pot of beans, and served breakfast. The Chalmers brothers were still there.

"Mr. Hooper asked Mr. Quincy if they could travel with us for a while," Miss Sky whispered to Jonas. She had brought the tin plates, cups, and tableware over from the wagon. "Mr. Quincy didn't seem happy about it, but he said yes." She giggled. "I heard him tell Daddy that those two boys are so ugly they'll scare off the wolves!"

"Reckon they will," Jonas agreed. After finding out the Chalmers boys were staying, he felt more miserable than ever.

"Ain't you eating, Jonas?" Mr. Quincy asked him.

"No, sir."

The wagon train leader looked at him sharply. "You ailing?"

"No, sir." He was ailing, terribly. His head hurt, his stomach hurt, and his soul hurt. But he couldn't talk about it yet—not even to Mr. Quincy.

Woodenly he washed and dried the breakfast things. He wasn't seeing the frying pan or the tin plates, though. He was seeing Tate jerking in pain and surprise as the master's bullet hit him, and Leola struggling and yelling out the truth with nobody believing her. He was seeing Esther and the others crying as the field hands dug a grave near Mama's—maybe in the place where he, Tate, and Leola had sat and talked not so long ago. He was seeing a plain rock for a gravestone, plain because nobody dared ask Master William or Miz Julia to have Tate's name etched on it. He was seeing Ebenezer strutting proudly around Hooper Hall, admiring his bag of money and basking in old Mr. Hooper's praise.

The horror Jonas felt was so big that he didn't know what to do with it. He couldn't beat it down to where it fit inside him, but he couldn't let it out. What did folks do with such pain? he wondered.

For a while that morning he drove the oxen. At first it was comforting to walk along beside the big, placid cattle and not have to talk. Then his heart started pounding as hard and fast as bare feet stamping on a dirt floor. Black patches crept over his vision so that the bright day began to look like night.

He turned and headed for the wagon. "Got to lie down, sir," he murmured to Mr. Quincy, stumbling past.

He heard the leader yell, "Hold up!" Then he was aware of people helping him climb into the wagon and settling him onto a pile of blankets. He was grateful for the help, for the softness of the blankets, and for the wagon canvas shielding him from the sun.

The sun, he thought, closing his eyes. Leola be working out in the sun now. Picking cotton down South. Or tobacco. Maybe she be picking tobacco. Just because she tried to stop Tate from doing something crazy.

"What's wrong with him, Daddy?" Miss Sky sounded worried.

"Probably a fever of some sort," Dr. Yoder replied. "Could be the ague, or maybe too much sun. Rest will be the best cure."

"He's just malingering." That was Master Percy's voice. "Needs a taste of the whip."

"Don't be ridiculous, Hooper!" Mr. Quincy snapped. "Can't you tell he's sick?"

"You reckon it's contagious?" whined Bud Chalmers. Nobody answered him.

Jonas was glad when everyone went away and it was quiet. Pretty soon, Mr. Quincy yelled, "Move out!" The wagon started rolling again, bumping its way across the prairie. Even on the pile of blankets, it was a bone-jarring, teeth-rattling experience. Jonas didn't mind, though, because it jolted the sobs out of him. Sobbing didn't do much to ease the pain in his heart, but it wore him out enough that he fell into a dreamless sleep.

When he awoke, it was dark, and there was a lantern inside the wagon. He sat up. Miss Sky was looking through the provisions.

"It's me," she said. "I'll fix supper. You go back to sleep."

"Thank you, miss," Jonas murmured.

He slept again. The next time he woke up it was because Mr. Quincy was hunkered down beside him, gently shaking him. "You need to eat, son. Here's some soup that Miss Sophronia made."

Jonas sat up and took the bowl and spoon Mr. Quincy held out to him. The soup had bacon and onions in it, and tasted good. He ate about half of it before the horror inside him closed off his throat.

"Go on and finish it," Mr. Quincy urged. In a lower voice, he added, "It ain't as good as your own cooking, but she worked hard on it."

Jonas tried to finish it so as not to hurt Miss Sky's feelings, but the lump in his throat was too big. "Sorry, sir," he said, handing the bowl back to Mr. Quincy. "That be all I can manage. Tell Miss Sophronia thank you."

"I'll do that," Mr. Quincy said. "By the way, you'll be glad to know that Dr. Yoder has ordered Mr. Hooper to stay away from you." He grinned. "Actually, I think he hinted that you might have something contagious."

"That was real kind of him," Jonas replied gratefully. He couldn't have abided Master Percy right then.

After sleeping all day and eating the soup, Jonas felt stronger. But in a way he wished he didn't, because now he had to ask himself the questions he didn't want to face: How could he go home and stand to be trained by Ebenezer? How could he bear to be Master William's manservant, knowing what the master had done to Tate and Leola?

And he had to ask himself the most awful question of all: Would he someday turn into the kind of servant that Ebenezer was—one who would betray his own people to please the master? Surely not! But maybe Ebenezer hadn't thought he'd ever become that way, either.

God, tell me what to do, he prayed silently. I don't want to be a manservant when I gets home, but I ain't got no choice.

At last he pulled the blanket around himself and tried

to sleep. Just as he was drifting off, a thought exploded in his head as brightly as a firecracker.

"I don't have to go home," he whispered. Tate had said that there were people in Kansas Territory who helped slaves get to Canada. Maybe he could find someone who would help him escape!

He stared up at the wagon canvas and thought. If he escaped to Canada, he'd never have to see Ebenezer or Master William again. He'd be beyond the reach of Master Percy's slapping hands, too.

But how would he find someone who would help him? And what would it be like to run away, knowing that he would be scared and lonely and would never see home again?

Jonas finally slept. When he awoke in the morning, his first thought was, Canada!

Before this, he had never understood Tate's longing to escape. But now he realized that once you started thinking about setting yourself free and living your own life, you couldn't rest. He'd heard folks at home call it "getting bit by the freedom bug." Now he was beginning to believe the freedom bug had bitten him hard, just like a big old horsefly.

Suddenly he heard angry voices coming from outside the wagon.

"I say it's time he gets back to work," Master Percy was saying.

"Mr. Hooper," replied Dr. Yoder, "I tell you, the boy must stay in bed."

"He's my slave, and he ought to be fixing our meals and waiting on my friends and me."

"Hooper," came Mr. Quincy's voice, "what the Sam Hill are you hollering about?"

"I want my slave boy out here doing his work, that's what!" snapped Master Percy. "And don't try to tell me he might have something contagious. If you believed that, you wouldn't be getting ready to go visit him. Dr. Yoder wouldn't be letting his little gal go into the wagon, either."

Mr. Quincy said firmly, "Listen to me, Hooper. Jonas ain't getting out of bed until the doctor says he's ready. Now you quit your yelling and go hitch up the oxen. I'm still the leader of this train, and I give the orders."

"Aw, you're as bad as my pa," Master Percy muttered as he stomped away.

Mr. Quincy climbed into the wagon. "Well, I see you're awake, young man."

"Yes, sir."

"Miss Sophronia is fixing breakfast. I can have her bring you something if you want. You need to keep your strength up."

"That'd be real nice, sir."

Mr. Quincy stood silently for a minute. Then he hunkered down beside Jonas's makeshift bed and asked, "You feel like talking a minute?"

"Yes, sir."

Slowly Mr. Quincy said, "Son, I know Henry Yoder says you've got the ague or a touch of sun, but I ain't so sure. Last time I saw somebody look like you do, it was a feller who'd just seen a scalping. He had that same kind of haunted, someplace-else look in his eye." He paused. "You ain't just seen a scalping, have you?"

"N-no, sir." Then, without planning to, he told Mr. Quincy about Tate and Leola. He saw the man's eyes fill with shock and anger.

When he'd finished, Mr. Quincy said nothing at first. Then he swore quietly and terribly, using oaths and words Jonas had never heard. He invoked the wrath of the Lord on Master William, cursed old Mr. Hooper's bodily organs, and consigned Ebenezer to everlasting hell.

"Sir," said Jonas, interrupting, "I don't know how I can bear to go back home. Master William aims to make me his manservant, and Ebenezer's the one who's supposed to train me."

That brought on a fresh round of swearing.

"Mr. Quincy!" Jonas said loud enough to be heard. When he had the man's attention, he lowered his voice. "I—I been thinking that maybe instead of going home I ought to light out for Canada."

Mr. Quincy raised his shaggy eyebrows in surprise. "Son, that sounds like the best idea I've heard in a long time."

"It does?" Jonas felt cheered.

"Sure does. Have you come up with a plan?"

"No, sir. But I recollect Tate saying that out here in Kansas Territory, there's folks that'll hide slaves and help them get to Canada. Do you think I could find me some of them folks?"

Mr. Quincy shook his head. "Not in these parts. There's people up in Lawrence and Topeka who'd be glad to help you, but they're a long ways off."

Jonas's heart was heavy with disappointment. "I ain't sure I could do it by myself. I wouldn't even know which way to start walking."

From outside a voice cried, "Mr. Quincy! Where are you? We need you to come look at an ox's hoof."

"Dang it all," muttered the wagon train leader. "I better go find out what the trouble is. You try to get some sleep, young feller. I'll see what kind of a plan I can concoct."

"Thank you, sir."

Mr. Quincy was going to help him! Jonas smiled to himself. He might really be going to Canada. He wished he knew more about it. Was it a country, or a town? How far away was it? Did you have to cross one of those wide oceans to get there? He decided he would ask Miss Sky. She'd probably know all about Canada.

It wasn't long before a head of gingery hair appeared at the back opening of the wagon. Miss Sky lifted a tray into the wagon and climbed in after it.

"I brought you some tea and biscuits," she said, carrying the tray over to Jonas. "I hope the biscuits are all right. The men didn't eat them as quick as they do yours."

They were about as light and fluffy as horseshoes, but Jonas told her they were fine.

"Oh, good," she said, looking relieved. She sat down on the wagon floor. "I heard Mr. Quincy tell Daddy that he plans to throw out those awful Chalmers brothers. He said he had a bad feeling about them at the start, but he didn't have any grounds for refusing to let them travel with us. Now he does, though, because they're always drinking and cutting up, and they refuse to pull guard duty."

"I'd be happy to see the last of them two," Jonas said. He took a sip of tea. "Miss Sky, do you suppose you could teach me to read a map?"

She nodded. "I'll come tonight and show you my geography book."

"You—you reckon you could come today at lunchtime?"

Miss Sky looked surprised. "Why, yes, I suppose so. Right now, I'd better get back and wash the dishes." She stood up and took Jonas's plate and cup. "Get some rest, and I'll see you at lunchtime."

The wagon train got under way soon afterward. It bumped and rattled for hours. Jonas dozed off and dreamed of Tate and Leola. Later, Miss Sky came into the wagon and said they'd crossed the Cottonwood River and were in buffalo country. "We haven't seen any buffalo yet," she told him, "but Mr. Quincy says we will soon."

She went over to her trunk, rummaged around, and pulled out a piece of paper and a thin, brown-covered book. She brought them to Jonas and sat down beside him. Carefully she unfolded the piece of paper. "This is from one of Daddy's guidebooks. It shows the western United States. This line is our route to the Rockies."

Jonas stared. A funny shape, outlined with gray shading, covered most of the sheet. On it were smooth black lines that dipped and curved; short, feathery gray lines that looked like furry caterpillars; and rough, wiggly lines with short lines trailing from them, like branches and twigs. Words and dots were scattered around. Some were in big letters that swooped up and down the page, and others were in small letters beside the dots.

Jonas was dismayed. How could he ever make sense of those twigs and caterpillars?

"I'm sorry, miss, but it don't look like nothing to me."

Miss Sky explained patiently. The gray fuzzy lines were the mountains, and the lines that looked like branches were rivers. The twigs were creeks. The dots were towns, and the writing beside them said their names. The big swooping words were the names of the states and territories.

"But how do you know them things be where the map say?" Jonas asked.

"Because the maps are made by explorers who go out and measure the distances and draw the rivers and such," Miss Sky replied.

To demonstrate, she drew a map of the wagon, showing where the trunks and provisions were. She said that maps always had north at the top and included a little scale showing how much distance an inch stood for. Jonas nodded. The idea of maps was starting to make sense. He watched excitedly as Miss Sky pointed out Missouri and Pikes Peak, and showed him where they were on the trail.

"We're heading west," she said. "You can tell that

when we're walking. The sun rises in the east, which is be-hind us, so in the morning it warms our backs. During the day, it crosses the sky from east to west. In the afternoon, it shines in our eyes because we're walking toward it. Then it sets in the west."

"I think I understand," Jonas said, fascinated. "Miss, which direction is Canada?"

"Canada? It's up north. I'll show you." She flipped through the geography book until she found the page she wanted. "It's this pink country. This green part is the top of the United States."

"So Canada be a country." Jonas was relieved to see that he wouldn't have to cross an ocean to get there. With one finger, he touched the pink land.

Miss Sky whispered, "Are you thinking of going there?"

"Thinking of it. I ain't sure yet."

"Oh, Jonas, I hope you do! Wait, I hear Daddy calling me. I'd better go."

"First, would you show me where the South be? It's where the cotton and tobacco grow."

Miss Sky turned the page to a map of what she said was the whole United States. It was divided into funny-shaped areas in different colors. Those areas were states and territories, Jonas learned. The pale greens, yellows, and pinks made him think of the mint, lemon, and rasp-berry creams Mama used to make.

"Here's the South." Miss Sky was pointing to the lower right-hand section of the map. Quickly she read him the names of the states: Alabama, Mississippi, Georgia, South Carolina . . .

Jonas had heard those names before. In the Big House, Master William and his guests bandied them about in their after-dinner talk of politics. In the slave quarters, the field hands spoke them in tones of fear and sorrow. Now Jonas wondered which one of those states Leola had gone to.

After Miss Sky left, Jonas slept for a while. When he awoke, he studied his alphabet letters and numbers. It was more important than ever that he know how to read, write, and count. He would need those skills when he was free. Free! He whispered the word. It made the same sound that a gentle breeze made.

That evening, Mr. Quincy brought him crackers and beef jerky.

"We couldn't start a cooking fire because of the rain," he explained. Then, in a lower voice, he said, "I came up with a plan for your escape."

"You did? What is it, sir?"

"It's pretty simple. When we get through digging for gold out in the mountains, you hide out in this wagon and go on to the state of California with the Yoders and me. Now," he added hastily, "Henry Yoder'll be mad as a hornet when he finds out you've stowed away. He thinks it's thievery to help a man's slaves escape. But if you hide until we're out on the trail, he won't have a choice but to let you stay with us till we reach California." He gave a short laugh. "I reckon he'll forgive me for it eventually."

"I hope so, sir," Jonas replied, feeling grateful and

humble. "This California. Is it a free state—one where I can live?" How wonderful, to be near Mr. Quincy and Miss Sky!

But the man was shaking his head. "It's a free state, but it ain't the place for you to roost. From what I hear, the people there don't like black folks and ain't very accommodating to them. They're even talking about passing a law to keep blacks out." Mr. Quincy looked Jonas in the eye. "Son, I hate to say it, but there ain't no state or territory in this country that'll welcome you. That's the sad truth. You'll have to head up to Canada, like you planned."

"Can I get there from California?"

"Sure can. Once you're in California, you can make your way to the coast and catch a boat on up to Canada. There's an island called Vancouver where I hear they're welcoming black people."

"You mean they *wants* us there?"

"The governor's inviting blacks to come settle the land. Might be just the place for you."

All evening, Jonas thought about Canada. It would be good to live with other former slaves and to be in a place where he was welcome. Surely he could find a job as a cook. Even people in Canada had to eat, didn't they? And maybe there'd be a school he could go to! Best of all, he would be free. Nobody could slap him, or humiliate him, or make him do things that his heart said were wrong.

Jonas nodded slowly. He wanted to go to Vancouver Island.

8

THINKING ABOUT CANADA AND FREEDOM GOT JONAS through the next day. He swore to Dr. Yoder that he felt strong enough to take on his chores, but there was still a hurting place in his heart when he thought about Tate and Leola.

As the group prepared to leave that morning, gusts of wind began blowing from the north. Within a few hours, it was so cold that the travelers had to get out their winter coats. When it started to rain, they donned India rubber ponchos over their coats. The Chalmers brothers, who were sticking to the Quincy train like burrs to a dog, had brought ponchos but no coats.

"It's summertime," whined Dag. "We figured it'd be hot out here."

His brother added, "Seemed foolish to load down our wagon with heavy coats."

Master Percy told them, "Don't worry. You just stay in your wagon and wrap blankets around you. My boy Jonas here will drive your mules."

Jonas gasped. "But, sir, I ain't never driven mules. Ain't sure I can—"

"You drive those mules, boy, and quit arguing with me!" Master Percy snapped.

Dr. Yoder overheard them. He said, "I forbid it, Mr. Hooper. The boy's the one who should be resting in a wagon, not the Chalmers brothers. Jonas, I insist that you get back in the wagon."

"This boy belongs to me!" Master Percy retorted. "I'm the one that gives him orders, and I'm ordering him to drive my friends' mules."

Dr. Yoder raised an eyebrow. "As I recall, the boy belongs to your father. He might not be pleased if he finds out his boy died of pneumonia while he was in your care."

Master Percy pressed his lips together and walked away. Jonas thankfully climbed back into the wagon, wrapped himself in blankets, and spent the day with a reading primer Miss Sky had loaned him.

When they stopped for the night, he decided he felt well enough to get up and make supper. He was rolling out bread dough on the fold-down table behind the wagon when he heard Mr. Quincy tell Dag and Bud Chalmers, "Boys, we need to have us a talk."

Jonas stopped working so he could listen. He caught the words ". . . haven't pulled guard duty . . . haven't done any chores . . . been getting drunk and cutting up." The brothers replied loudly and angrily, but their words were so slurred with drink that Jonas couldn't understand them.

Mr. Quincy's final words came across clearly. "We'll be parting ways tomorrow. I'll give you a choice: you can stay in camp all day and let us get ahead of you, or you can go ahead and we'll wait here for a day."

"And what if we don't want to do neither one?" came Dag's voice.

"Then you'll be tied to a wagon and given twenty lashes each with a bullwhip," Mr. Quincy pronounced.

Dag and Bud yelled with rage. When Master Percy found out what was happening, he added his voice to theirs. Mr. Quincy just quietly repeated, "We part ways peacefully, or you get twenty lashes and are left behind. It's up to you."

The next morning the two brothers sulkily agreed to leave.

"We'll be the ones to go on ahead, though," Dag told Mr. Quincy.

Bud said, "That's right. We ain't going to sit here and waste time while you get a day's march on us."

"Fine," Mr. Quincy replied. "We'll stay here in camp until tomorrow."

Jonas was relieved to know that the Chalmers boys were leaving, but he soon became worried, as well. After breakfast, he was passing by their wagon and heard them talking inside. He stopped and held his breath, listening.

"We'll make that old man sorry he threw us out," Dag said.

"We won't do anything real bad, will we?" Bud sounded nervous. "I don't want to get hanged or nothing."

"You think I'm stupid? We ain't gonna get hanged." Dag snorted. "I declare, you ain't got the grit God gave a mouse."

"That ain't true!"

"Is so. I'm the only man around here with any gumption. Percy ain't much better than you are. He's even scared of his pa!"

"You letting Perce in on our plans?"

"Nah! Ain't no reason to. Come on, we better hitch up the mules."

Jonas hurried away. After the brothers had left camp and started down the trail, he told Mr. Quincy what he had heard.

The wagon train leader swore. "I'm grateful to you for letting me know. Those durned fools—they'll probably run off the livestock, or overturn our wagon." Mr. Quincy patted Jonas's shoulder and said, "Don't you worry, son. We outnumber them, and we're a whole lot smarter than them."

In the afternoon, the men went on a buffalo hunt. They had been seeing herds of the great, brown, furry beasts at a distance, and Jonas had learned to cook over patties of dried buffalo dung—or "buffalo chips," as Mr. Quincy called them—now that firewood was so scarce.

While the men were gone, Jonas and Miss Sky sat in the wagon and went over alphabet letters. He learned up to *L*. Then he asked, "Miss, would you mind showing me that map again? The one with the pretty colors?"

He pored over that map, fascinated. The book had other maps, too, showing each state close up. It also had sketches of scenes in different places. The ones of Canada showed snowstorms and sleighs.

"Do you reckon it snows in Canada all the time?" he asked, worried.

"No, probably just in the winter," she replied. Then she peered at him closely and said, "Jonas, you still seem awful interested in Canada. You don't have to tell me if you don't want to—but have you decided to go there?"

He hesitated only a second before telling her the whole story. She cried when he told her about Tate and Leola, and swore to help him any way she could. "I'm *so* glad you're not going back home," she said fervently, "and I'll help you hide when the time comes. Mr. Quincy's right about Daddy. He'll be angry at first, but he'll get over it."

She showed him how he would sail up the California coastline to Canada. The map didn't show Vancouver Island, the place where black folks were welcome, but Miss Sky said she was pretty sure it was on the west coast. When Jonas looked at the map, he thought about how odd and sad it was that one of these days he'd be clear up there in Canada, the Yoders and Mr. Quincy would be in California, Esther would be in Missouri, and Leola would be down South. As for Tate, Jonas prayed he was in heaven.

After a while, they were interrupted by the whoops of the men returning from the hunt. "We bagged us a buffalo!" they cried happily. "Mr. Quincy and a few others are out there carving it up. We'll all have steaks for supper tonight!"

Jonas was glad that only the carved-up meat, not the whole buffalo, was brought in. He knew he couldn't bear to see anything that had been shot dead. He didn't have much heart to eat the steaks, which Mr. Quincy fried up that evening, even though the rest of the party ate voraciously. Master Percy ate three steaks and bragged that he'd be the next to kill a buffalo.

The following day they crossed a toll bridge over the Little Arkansas River. As they continued westward, they met more and more men who were returning home from the gold fields. A few had found some gold, but most had found only hard conditions. "Ain't no gold pieces out there," one said. "The whole thing's a hoax. Do yourselves a favor and turn around before you get any farther."

Many men, called "go-backs," were doing just that— giving up and going home. Someone said, "We've heard too many discouraging stories. Besides, we're busted— tired, sick, and out of provisions. We can't go on."

One night Jonas heard Master Percy asking another man, "You think those fellas are right? That the talk of gold is just a hoax, and we ought to turn around?"

Jonas didn't hear the reply. He prayed that Master

Percy wouldn't ever decide to call it quits and join a train heading home.

On Monday, they reached the big bend of the Arkansas River, which Mr. Quincy said was a landmark on the trail. The water was sandy, but it was cool and tasted good. Best of all, the weather was warm and clear again, and they found a place in the river that was deep enough to bathe in. Miss Sky got to go first, while her daddy stood guard. Jonas went later with the men. Like everyone else, he was covered with trail dust and mosquito bites. It felt wonderful to stand in the neck-deep water! He didn't even mind having to scrub Master Percy's back.

They soon started seeing more Indians. Unlike the Kaw, these had long, straight hair and wore soft deerskin shirts, trousers, and shoes. Mr. Quincy said they were from the Kiowa and Arapaho tribes, and were probably in temporary camps while they hunted buffalo. They came begging for food, and Mr. Quincy had Jonas take them some sugar, crackers, and tea. They were as fascinated by Jonas as he was by them, and liked to touch his skin and hair. Every time they'd finger his hair, he'd cry, "Mr. Quincy!"

The Indians would laugh, and even Mr. Quincy would chuckle. "They ain't going to scalp you," he'd say. "They're just curious. They've probably never seen a black person before." After a while, Jonas got used to it and didn't mind so much.

The wagon train followed the Arkansas River now. Mr. Quincy said they wouldn't part company with it until a few days before they hit the gold fields. Jonas smiled when he heard that. It made him feel that he was getting close to freedom. To be sure he was ready for it, he had been studying his alphabet whenever he could. He was learning to read now. He knew six words: *some, come, cat, hat, look,* and *cook.* With a little work, he could puzzle out others.

One day at lunchtime, he looked at the wagon canvas and, to his amazement, he could read what it said. "Ho for Pikes Peak," he whispered. He stood there grinning at that dirty old canvas until Master Percy snapped at him to quit gazing into space and cut some more bread.

The next landmark on the trail was Pawnee Rock, which they reached that Wednesday, the first day of June. It was a huge, sunburnt bluff rising straight up out of the flat, scrubby land. They could see it for miles, and even though it was a little ways off the trail, the men proposed going there.

"I reckon we got time," Mr. Quincy said.

They took some apples and leftover biscuits and scrambled up the rock to have a picnic. It turned out that even though the rock looked hard and black from a distance, it was actually red sandstone, soft enough to carve into with a knife. It was covered with the names of people who had been there. The men in the Quincy train added theirs, as did Miss Sky. She wrote out her whole first name, Sophronia, so people would know she was a girl.

"There are a few girls' names up here, but none on this part of the rock," she said smugly.

That gave Jonas an idea. He told Miss Sky, "If you wouldn't mind sharing with another gal, I'd like to put Leola's name up here. Hers and Tate's."

"I'd be proud to share with her," Miss Sky replied.

While she kept watch, Jonas borrowed her penknife and etched *JONAS* into the rock. Then, with her help on the spelling, he added *TATE* and *LEOLA*.

"They'd be mighty pleased," Miss Sky told him.

Jonas said, "With their names up here soaring over the land, it kind of seems like they be free. Like birds."

Then Mr. Quincy started hollering that it was time to go. They had to cross the Pawnee River, which ran into the Arkansas, before dark. Jonas said a quick prayer before he and Miss Sky joined the others. They got back on the trail and started west once again. Every so often, Jonas glanced back at Pawnee Rock rising over the plains. He felt as if he'd left a piece of himself up there.

Among the other wagon trains on the trail were several of the long, merchant ones bound for Santa Fe. Jonas wondered whether one might belong to Mr. Rulo. Sure enough, that evening as he was fixing supper at their campsite on the banks of the Pawnee River, they heard a shout: "Is Jeremiah Quincy's train camped here?" and there appeared a big bear of a man on a buckskin horse.

"I can't stay long," he told them. "We've got to set out early tomorrow morning. We're behind schedule, so we need to make the Middle Crossing of the Arkansas River on Sunday." He grinned at Jonas. "But I reckon I could stay long enough to have some of that good-smelling brew you're making."

"It's a soup I thought up, sir," Jonas said. "You're welcome to have some. I got biscuits baking, too."

"Why, thank you, son. I'd be mighty happy to stay for supper."

Mr. Rulo dismounted and hobbled his buckskin, then joined the others by the campfire. Jonas set out the biscuits and coffee and served the soup, which he'd made with buffalo meat, beans, and dried onions. Everybody praised it highly. Even Master Percy said it was tasty, although he scolded Jonas for not making more.

As they ate, Mr. Rulo told them about his train's preparations for the Jornada del Muerto. "We have to check over the wagons to make sure they're in shape for the trip, and fill up all our water kegs. On Saturday night, the cooks will be up until all hours baking bread, to make sure we don't run out."

"How long will the Jornada take?" Miss Sky asked.

"Well, missy, we'll cross the Arkansas River on Sunday and rest until sundown. If we travel all night and all day Monday, we'll make the Cimarron River on Tuesday."

Mr. Rulo ate two bowls of soup and several biscuits, then said he had to head back to his own train. As Jonas watched him and Mr. Quincy shake hands, he thought he saw a wistful look in the older man's eyes. Maybe, he thought, Mr. Quincy wished he were still young enough to cross the desert and have a wild adventure, too.

After Mr. Rulo had gone, Jonas and Miss Sky got water from the Pawnee River and boiled it for dish washing. As they did the dishes, she taught him, in whispers, how to spell *tea*, *beans*, and *three*.

"What about *free*, miss?" he asked. "That sounds a lot like those words."

She spelled *free*, and he spelled it after her slowly, savoring the sound of the letters. *Free* was getting to be the most important word in his life.

"Do you think you can learn these by tomorrow?" Miss Sky asked him.

Jonas replied, "Can't do much studying tonight. Master Percy got the early guard duty. I'll keep spelling them in my head, though, while I'm trying to fall asleep."

Master Percy wasn't happy that there were only two men on his shift of guard duty.

"I've heard there are Indian tipis nearby," he told Mr. Quincy. "I think you ought to double the guard tonight."

Mr. Quincy shook his head. "That ain't necessary. Your partner's Mr. Graham, and he's a steady, capable fellow. If there's any trouble, just give a holler."

Later, as Jonas lay in his bedroll, spelling his new words to himself, he watched Master Percy pace back and forth, a rifle over one shoulder. He constantly stopped and glanced nervously in all directions. One time he abruptly yelled, "Who's there?" and stood for a moment, listening. Apparently he didn't get a reply, because he walked on.

Jonas's last thought before falling asleep was, If something's gonna happen tonight, I sure hope it don't happen on Master Percy's watch.

When Jonas heard a bang, he first thought he'd had another dream about Tate. Then he heard Mr. Quincy hollering and cussing at the top of his lungs. Quickly he threw back his cover and jumped up. Dr. Yoder was rushing over, clad in long underwear, and Miss Sophronia was behind him, holding a wrapper close around her. Other men were coming, too, some of them brandishing guns.

Mr. Quincy was sitting on the ground, rocking back and forth, clutching one arm. Master Percy was kneeling beside him with a lantern, his rifle on the ground.

"Jeremiah, what happened?" asked Dr. Yoder.

Panting and glassy-eyed with pain, Mr. Quincy said, "I came out of my tent 'cause I woke up and heard the oxen making noise. I saw Mr. Graham heading over that way. I was going to join him when somebody shot me. He was behind that stand of elms. Mr. Graham's gone hunting for him."

"Some of you men go help Graham," Dr. Yoder directed.

Master Percy was pale and shaky. "I didn't see anything, honest! I heard a shot and came running over and found Quincy here."

The doctor said, "Quit jawing and hold the lantern steady."

"Y-you might want to get somebody else to help you,"

Master Percy replied nervously. "My stomach's acting funny. I'm not used to seeing blood."

The doctor sighed. "Hooper, you're worthless. Sophronia, take the lantern from him."

She took the lantern, and Master Percy staggered off, looking sick. He motioned for Jonas to follow, but Jonas stayed where he was. Dr. Yoder knelt on the ground to examine Mr. Quincy's arm. Jonas heard the doctor say, "It looks kind of messy, Jeremiah, but I'll try to remove the bullet."

"All right." The older man sighed resignedly. "Just bring me some whiskey, and get your little gal out of earshot so's I can cuss proper."

Dr. Yoder said quietly, "Sophronia and Jonas, bring me a bottle of whiskey."

Glad for something to do, Jonas ran to the wagon with Miss Sky.

"Do you think he'll be all right?" Jonas asked her as they looked for the whiskey.

"I think so. He's pretty tough." But Miss Sky's voice shook.

There were more yells from outside, and Jonas and Miss Sky clambered out of the wagon to see what was happening. Mr. Graham and the others were bringing two surly-looking men into camp. Both men had guns nuzzling their backs and their hands in the air.

"Look who we found running off from the direction of those elm trees," said Mr. Graham.

The two men were Dag and Bud Chalmers.

9

AG CHALMERS ADMITTED THAT HE HAD SHOT MR. Quincy, but swore it had been an accident. He and Bud had been coming to visit Percy, he said, and had thought Mr. Quincy was an Indian getting set to steal the livestock.

Dr. Yoder looked at him with disgust. "You expect us to believe you were paying a call at that time of night? Anyway, you shouldn't have been here at all—you knew you weren't welcome in our camp." He shook his head. "I think it's clear that you shot him on purpose because he threw you off the train."

There was a lot of cursing and hollering, and, in the end, the two brothers were tied to a wagon wheel for the rest of the night. They called on Master Percy to set them free, but he just looked scared and said, "Sorry, boys. I reckon it wasn't such a good idea for you to be shooting in the dark."

After the Chalmers brothers had been secured, Dr. Yoder chose a couple of men to help him and set about removing the bullet from Mr. Quincy's arm. The midnight-to-morning guards took their posts, and everyone else went back to bed.

Jonas got into his bedroll, but he couldn't sleep. He kept hearing Mr. Quincy groaning, and wished there was something he could do. He thought of what a good friend the man was. He remembered how Mr. Quincy had shaken his hand when they'd first met and had asked his advice on provisions, as though they were equals. And, even though he felt selfish, he couldn't help but worry about his escape plan. What would he do if Mr. Quincy had to turn back and go home?

Jonas dozed fitfully for a while, and awoke when one of the guards shook him and said it was time to fix breakfast. As he took the provisions from the back of the wagon, he saw that Mr. Quincy was lying asleep on a pile of thick blankets inside. He tried to work quietly: he kept the pots and pans from clanging, and he made tea instead of coffee so there wouldn't be any bean-grinding to awaken the injured man.

Dr. Yoder came to breakfast, but all he would say was, "We'll have a meeting of the whole camp this morning. I'll talk about Jeremiah's condition then."

"He won't die, will he?" asked Master Percy.

"No," Dr. Yoder replied. He smiled grimly. "Don't

worry, Mr. Hooper. Your friends won't get hanged for murder."

Master Percy gulped and got very busy eating his beans and bacon.

Later, as Jonas was washing the breakfast things, he felt a hand on his shoulder. For a moment, he thought a miracle had happened and it was Mr. Quincy. But when he looked around, Master Percy was standing there, a strained smile on his lips and an anxious look in his pale gray eyes.

Quietly the master said, "Say, boy, I got a proposition for you. If you swear you won't tell my father anything about our meeting up with Dag and Bud, I'll give you a nice big gold piece when we get to Pikes Peak. How about it?"

Jonas wanted to punch him in the face. Don't hit him, he warned himself. Just act like a good little servant, and don't give him any reason to watch you closer.

He made himself smile and say, "That's real kind of you, Master Percy. I s'pose in that case I can see fit to keep a secret or two."

"Good." Master Percy sounded relieved. "You remind me, once we get there."

He started to leave, then turned around. "You know, Jonas, you're a fine boy. I can see why my papa chose you to be his manservant."

"Thank you, sir." Jonas kept his hands in the dishwater so the master couldn't see that they were shaking with anger.

Soon Dr. Yoder chose a meeting place and called everyone over. Jonas nodded to Miss Sky. She looked as anxious as he felt.

"First of all," Dr. Yoder said, addressing the camp, "Jeremiah is resting comfortably. He'll live, and I don't think he'll lose his arm. Still, it was a bad wound and there's a chance that infection will set in. At the least, he'll need to stay here for a few days, to rest."

He took a deep breath. "What I propose is that you all consider hitching up with another wagon train to go on to the gold fields. My daughter and I will stay with Jeremiah. If he does all right, we'll continue, traveling in slow stages. If he doesn't do all right, we'll have to either get him back East to civilization or try to make it to Bent's Fort, which is about two weeks down the trail, and stay there a spell."

There was a buzz of talk. Someone cried, "What about the Chalmers boys?"

Dr. Yoder said, "The other wagon leaders and I will decide that."

After the meeting, Jonas got the doctor's permission to sit with Mr. Quincy awhile. His heart felt heavy when he saw how pale and weak the injured man looked.

"Morning, Jonas," Mr. Quincy murmured, not raising his head. "Guess you tried to warn me. I didn't think those no-good skunks would pull something like this. I figured they'd just try to stampede the oxen or steal some food."

Jonas said, "You rest, sir. I'll sit here a spell in case you need anything."

"That's kindly of you." Mr. Quincy's eyes were shut.

Jonas stayed with him until Miss Sky peeked in the front opening of the wagon.

"Daddy's met with the other leaders," she said softly. "He's getting everybody together to tell us what's to be done with the Chalmers brothers."

Mr. Quincy was sleeping, so Jonas left quietly and joined the others.

"Here's what we've decided," Dr. Yoder told the group. "We can't punish the Chalmers boys, since we can't prove they had planned to shoot Jeremiah. All we can do is let them go with a warning that they'll be shot on sight if they ever come to our camp again. They'll be heading out later today." He looked at Master Percy. "Mr. Hooper, we've decided you'll have to leave with them."

Jonas stared at Dr. Yoder. What would happen to *him* if Master Percy had to leave?

"But—but—" said Master Percy. "That's not fair! It wasn't my fault."

"I know you weren't aware of the plan to shoot Quincy," Dr. Yoder replied. "I asked the Chalmers boys if you were, and Dag said no. He said he hadn't told you because he knew you wouldn't have the nerve to go along with it."

Master Percy's face turned bright red, and his mouth opened and closed a couple of times. It was the first time Jonas had ever seen him at a loss for words.

"Still," Dr. Yoder continued, "even if you didn't know what they were planning to do, you were involved. You're the one who let those boys join our train to begin with. Besides, they insist that the purpose of their visit last night was to pay a call on you. We can't take a chance on their paying any more such calls. Anyway, you and your boy will be allowed to take your shares of the provisions when you leave. Someone will help you—"

Miss Sky interrupted. "But, Papa, you can't make Jonas leave! He isn't to blame."

"I know he isn't, honey," said Dr. Yoder, "but he belongs to Mr. Hooper."

Jonas listened, stunned. He was being sent off with Master Percy and the Chalmers brothers. He would have to leave his only two friends, Mr. Quincy and Miss Sky, and his reading lessons. And, dear Lord, how would he ever escape and get to Canada now?

Master Percy cried, "I can't go with Dag and Bud! Their wagon's too small. And what if we get lost and run out of food and water?"

"I've told you our decision, Mr. Hooper," the doctor said firmly. "You'll leave today, as soon as your trunks and provisions have been moved."

Two of the men marched Master Percy off to the wagon, to start moving his things. Jonas and Miss Sky ran to Dr. Yoder.

"Please let me stay here, sir," Jonas pleaded. "I'll cook for you, and drive the oxen, and help look after Mr. Quincy, and—and do anything you need me to."

"Papa, let him stay!" begged Miss Sky. "You *know* he'll be in danger if he sets off with those men. Please don't make him go!"

Dr. Yoder sighed and ran a hand across his face. "Sophronia, I don't want him to go, but I have no choice. I'm sorry, Jonas. If you didn't belong to Mr. Hooper, I'd be only too happy for you to stay with us. As it is, under the law, you're considered his property. If I tried to keep you here, he could rightfully accuse me of stealing."

"But isn't there a way—" Miss Sky began.

"No, Sophronia. I'm sorry, Jonas," her father repeated, and walked away.

Jonas and Miss Sky looked at each other.

"Miss, I can't go with them," Jonas whispered. "If I do, either they'll beat me to death or we'll get lost and die. 'Sides, how will I *ever* get to Canada? I might not be able to find you once we get to the gold fields."

"If we get there at all," Miss Sky said. "Maybe Mr. Quincy can help us."

Slowly Jonas shook his head. "Mr. Quincy ain't in no shape to help. We got to work this out on our own."

"Let's go sit down by the river and talk," said Miss Sky. She tried to smile. "Don't worry, Jonas. We'll think of something."

The Pawnee was a pretty, bubbling stream that sparkled in the sunlight, but it was flanked by dreary, scrub-covered hills and some scattered clumps of elm and ash trees. Gazing at it made Jonas long for the beautiful, green-shaded little Blackwater River at home, where he'd once fished with Tate.

He suddenly felt like a tired, hopeless old man.

"Maybe," Miss Sky ventured, "you could find somebody else on the train who would hide you and take you on to the gold fields."

Jonas thought. "No, miss. There ain't nobody I know, 'cept to say 'evening' and 'morning' to when we meet, or maybe give them some milk if they're running low. Can't ask a man to hide me when we ain't no better acquainted than that."

"No, I suppose not. Maybe you'll have a chance to run away once you're on the trail with Mr. Hooper and the Chalmers brothers."

"But where'll I go then?" Jonas asked bleakly. "Can't make it to the gold fields on my own. Can't ask strangers in another train to take me all that way, neither."

They both sat silently for a minute. A bird cried harshly.

Another train, thought Jonas absently. If only he knew someone . . .

"Miss Sky!" he cried. "What about Mr. Rulo? He'd help me!"

She grimaced. "Yes, except that he isn't going to the gold fields or California. He's going in the other direction, down to— Wait a minute!" Her face lit up. "Mexico! That's a different country, like Canada. I bet they don't have slavery there."

"You think I could find Mr. Rulo's train?"

"He was here just last night. That means he's only a day ahead of us. I think you could catch up with him be-fore—"

"Before he gets to the Jornada." Jonas's heart raced. If he couldn't catch up with Mr. Rulo by then, he'd have to make that Journey of the Dead Man by himself, on foot, with only what he could carry.

He could see from Miss Sky's eyes that she had realized the same thing.

"He said he wouldn't reach the Jornada until Sunday," she said quickly. "This is only Thursday. I'm sure you can find him in time! All you have to do is follow the river. Not this one, the Arkansas. I'll draw you a map."

Jonas thought fast. "Guess I can take some beef jerky, dried fruit, and crackers. Maybe some biscuits, too. And I be needing something to carry water in."

Miss Sky nodded. "I'll get you a canteen, and you can fill it in the river."

"When do you reckon I should leave?"

"Tonight, after Mr. Hooper and the Chalmers brothers are asleep. You'd better walk all night if you want to catch Mr. Rulo in time."

Jonas was trembling with excitement. He was going to escape that very night!

"We should get back to camp," Miss Sky said, standing up.

"Hope it take them a while to move Master Percy's belongings," Jonas told her. "I got a lot to think about."

To keep from disturbing Mr. Quincy more than necessary, Master Percy's trunks and his and Jonas's shares of the provisions were being loaded from their wagon into one of the others in the train. From that, they would be transferred to the Chalmers brothers' wagon, which was nearby. Dr. Yoder supervised the procedure.

Master Percy was watching sullenly. When he saw Jonas, he snarled, "I wondered where you'd gotten off to, you lazy little fool. You ought to be helping carry the provisions over to the other wagon."

"Here, Jonas," said Dr. Yoder. "You can take the sacks of sugar, tea, and salt."

"Yes, sir." Jonas scooped them up. "Sir, do you mind if I keep that tin of powdered yeast I use for the biscuits? Miss Sky don't need it. She use baking soda."

"What? Oh, yes, you may keep it," the doctor replied, handing it to him.

"Thank you, sir." Jonas added the tin to his load. He would need it in order to make biscuits for Mr. Rulo on the trail to Mexico.

As he was loading sacks and tins into the other wagon, a terrible thought hit him. What if Mr. Rulo didn't want him joining his train? But he'd said more than once that he wished Jonas were his cook.

Still, Jonas knew that even kindhearted people didn't always mean what they said.

When he voiced his fears to Miss Sky, she whispered, "Of course he'll let you join his train! Even if he didn't like your cooking, he wouldn't leave you stranded—and I'm sure he wouldn't give you back to Mr. Hooper."

Too soon, Master Percy's things were loaded.

"Say your farewells quick, boy," he said. "We need to

get my belongings to Dag and Bud's wagon and load them up before it gets dark."

"Won't take long, sir."

Jonas went to say goodbye to Mr. Quincy and found him awake.

"Sure wish you weren't having to leave," Mr. Quincy said weakly. "Ain't fair, ain't fair at all. But rest assured, I'll do all I can to find you when we get to the gold fields."

"Yes, sir." Jonas quickly decided not to say anything about running off with Mr. Rulo. Miss Sky could tell him later. He reached out and pressed the man's hand. "Thank you, sir."

"Best of luck to you, son," Mr. Quincy murmured, his eyes closing.

Miss Sky climbed into the wagon.

"Daddy gave him some medicine to make him sleep," she whispered. "Don't worry, Jonas. We'll take care of him."

From outside, they heard Master Percy yelling, "Where'd that durn boy get to?"

"I better go," Jonas said. But leaving was harder than anything he'd ever done. It was even harder than leaving home had been.

"Wait." Miss Sky dug hastily in her pocket, then held out a folded piece of paper. "This is a map I drew, showing your path. I traced it from one of Daddy's. I—I hope it'll help. And don't forget your alphabet and vocabulary lists."

"I got them," Jonas said, and put the map in his pocket. "Sky, when Mr. Quincy's stronger, tell him my plan. Otherwise, he'll come hunting for me."

She nodded, then gave a weak giggle. "Do you realize you just called me Sky without saying Miss?"

Jonas grinned. "Guess I did, Miss—I mean, Sky."

Master Percy appeared at the back of the wagon. "Dang it all, boy, you get yourself down here before I come in and box your ears! Everybody's waiting on you."

"Yes, sir."

It was time to say goodbye, but he couldn't make himself do it. Finally Sky said softly, "You better go now, Jonas," and turned away. He knew she was crying.

"Goodbye," he whispered. "I won't ever forget you or Mr. Quincy."

Then he made himself climb down from the wagon and join Master Percy.

10

THE MEN KEPT JONAS BUSY ALL EVENING. FIRST THEY wanted a supper of pancakes and bacon, and then they wanted a second pot of coffee. While they drank their coffee, they snapped at him. Every couple of minutes it was, "Boy, bring us a box of cigars!" "Hey, you, boy, ain't you polished our boots yet?" or "Boy, do something to quiet them mules!"

He took advantage of every chance to prepare for his escape. When he went to the river to get water for dish washing, he filled his canteen. As he put away the tinware after supper, he rolled up the leftover pancakes in a clean towel and put them in his flour sack. Later, when he climbed into the wagon to get the cigars for the men, he added dried apples, crackers, and an extra flannel shirt to his sack. He wished he could take his coat to guard against the night chill, but it was too heavy and bulky.

After his flour sack and canteen were safely stashed behind the provisions, there was nothing to do but wait for the men to go to sleep. Jonas had a bad moment when Master Percy asked, "Aren't we going to set a guard tonight?" But the Chalmers boys laughed.

"Sure, Perce, you stay up and guard us," Dag joshed.

Master Percy replied, "I'm too tired to shoot straight."

Finally, after Jonas had put up their tents for them, they went to bed. He lay in his bedroll under the wagon, pretending to sleep, until he heard their snores. Then he got up and went quietly to the wagon. A mule hee-hawed, making him freeze in his tracks, but the men didn't wake up.

He got his flour sack and canteen, eased himself down from the wagon, and walked away. Soon he was padding down the trail in the moonlight. With every step he expected to hear Master Percy yell, "Hey, boy!" but all was quiet. On three sides of him, the plains stretched to the horizon, then blended invisibly into the night sky. On his left side, low-lying brush and clumps of elm trees showed where the land fell to the river.

He had escaped! But instead of feeling elated and heady with freedom, he felt terrified. He was alone in this vast, wild land, and there was no going back. "God, see me through this night and help me be brave," he whispered. Then he wondered, Could God hear him, or were his words lost in the emptiness of the plains?

Wolves howled and a buffalo bellowed. Overhead, a falling star made a bright streak through the sky. Hadn't

Mama once said that a falling star meant somebody had died?

Mama! Sadness gripped his heart as he realized he'd never visit her grave again. Never see Esther, or the kitchen, or his attic again. Never see Sky or Mr. Quincy again, either. Running away sure meant a lot of goodbyes.

He reached the Arkansas River and turned westward. The nighttime desert was alive! Rabbits bounded across the trail. Antelopes, hearing Jonas, quit their grazing and sprang away. Farther off, packs of gray wolves crept and skulked. Two Indians silently rode by. A small band of wild horses galloped past, frolicking and tossing their manes. All the movement made Jonas feel as jumpy as a drop of water on a hot frying pan.

To take his mind off his fears, he thought about Mexico—about how someday he'd eat from a silver plate, have a house with an open space in the middle, dance at a *fandango*. When those thoughts went stale, he recited his alphabet letters and reviewed his new spelling words. It seemed a lifetime ago that Sky had written *tea*, *beans*, *three*, and *free*. He looked at the words now and wanted to weep with loneliness.

He spelled his words for a mile or so, but he stopped whispering them when he passed a large wagon train. Low voices and the orange glow of a cigarette tip told him that men were awake and on guard.

Then he came to a fork in the trail and panicked, wondering which way to go. But he could hear Sky saying, "All you have to do is follow the river."

Jonas walked and walked. Won't this night ever end? he wondered. Finally the sky acquired a milky tone to its blackness. Gradually it turned the shade of white clothes washed with blueing. In a Santa Fe train he passed, the cooks were fixing breakfast. What he wouldn't have given for a cup of coffee and some of that bacon he smelled! He made do with some beef jerky, a pancake, and a drink of water.

Soon the sun was creeping over the horizon, and people were back on the trail for another day's journey. Jonas had planned to find a hiding place and sleep in the daytime, but he decided to keep walking as long as he could. Every step, he told himself, would take him farther from Master Percy and closer to Mr. Rulo.

After much thought, he came up with a story to tell the people he met on the trail: he would say that part of his wagon train had gotten separated from the rest and that he was taking messages back and forth. It wasn't long before he got to try it out. The first train he caught up with was a short one, with only three wagons. The ox driver of the rearmost returned his nod.

"You out here by yourself, boy?" he asked.

Jonas made himself grin. "Just for now, sir. My party got separated a ways back and I be taking a message up the line." He shook his head, laughing. "They using me for a—what do you call that thing that sends messages?"

"A telegraph?" The man chuckled. "I guess they are."

Jonas ran ahead, trying to look like a happy boy on an errand. Lord bless Sky and Mr. Quincy, he thought. Because of them, he could look white folks in the eye and fool them into thinking he was free.

He told the same story to everyone he passed. Only one person, a sour-faced man with a gray beard, looked suspicious.

"What's your name, boy?" the man asked, his eyes narrowed.

Jonas's heart pounded. Could word of his escape have gotten out by now? He thought fast and answered, "Why— it be Benson, sir! Quincy Benson. I be with Mr.—uh, Mr. Tate's wagon train."

The man just grunted, and Jonas hurried on before he could ask any more questions.

"Quincy Benson," he said to himself, liking the sound of it. "Jonas Quincy Benson."

That would be his new name, his free name. No more Jonas Hooper. Now that he was free, he'd call himself who he was: Ben's son. He'd take his middle name from the other man who had helped make him, Mr. Quincy.

It felt good to have his own name.

He walked all day. By evening he was exhausted, hungry, and growing anxious. Shouldn't he have reached Mr. Rulo's train by now? Finally he got up his courage and approached the men of a Santa Fe train that had stopped early.

"Begging your pardon, sirs," he said casually. "Wondered if you could help me. I be looking for a man named Jack Rulo. He's a wagon master of—"

"Yeah, we know Jack," said one fellow. He had lank

blond hair and face stubble that was nearly beard length. He took a drag on his cigarette, tapped off the ashes onto the ground, and asked, "What's your business with him?"

Jonas said, "I got a message for him from my own wagon master."

"You looking for old Jack Rulo?" A young, dark-haired fellow pouring a cup of coffee looked up. "He usually takes the Dry Route."

Jonas's heart sank. "The Dry Route, sir? Reckon I don't know what that is."

"You *are* a greenhorn, aren't you?" The dark-haired man grinned and walked over. "The Dry Route runs north of here. It cuts off about thirty miles, and meets up with this trail a little ways west of here. If you stay on this trail, you'll have a chance of meeting him before he crosses the river. I believe he likes to take one of the Middle Crossings."

"That's what my boss said." Jonas tried to sound casual, but he was dismayed. He hadn't known there was more than one Middle Crossing. "Thank you kindly."

As he went on his way, the stubbly-faced man called, "Better watch out for the Indians, boy! They'd just love to add a black, woolly scalp to their belts."

He laughed uproariously. Jonas pretended not to have heard. He wished he *hadn't* heard, because the words sent a thrill of terror through him.

So Mr. Rulo was on another route, and he might take any one of several river crossings! Jonas gave a sigh. Back at Mr. Quincy's camp, this plan had seemed simple. Now

Jonas wondered whether he'd ever find Mr. Rulo. What would he do if he didn't? His food wouldn't last forever, and sooner or later Master Percy would catch up with him.

That night was as terrifying as the one before it. Across the river, white hills of sand shimmered, looking eerily like summer snowdrifts. Packs of shadowy gray wolves slid past, closer than Jonas liked. One wolf turned to growl at him and he threw a rock at it.

The Indian men he'd seen last night reappeared, and tonight they rode closer to the trail. Jonas tried not to look at them, but after a while he sneaked a peek. They were big, tall men, but they rode their ponies with an easy grace. When they saw him looking at them, they called out to him and motioned for him to come closer. He ran away, his heart thumping. He wondered whether it was true that they prized Negro scalps.

After a while he got so sleepy that he started wandering off the trail. Once he stumbled into a patch of those devilish plants called prickly pear. The cactus needles pierced his pants and stuck into his legs like red-hot daggers, making him cry out. He limped down to the river and sat in the shallow water, bathing his wounds. Then he lay down to rest. When he woke up, he was stiff and sore, but he didn't dare sleep longer. He ate a pancake and the last of the dried apples, then started walking again.

He whispered, "I be Jonas Quincy Benson, the famous cook, going to Mexico." The words made him feel brave for a moment, but then they turned to dust and blew away.

He thought, Maybe I just be Jonas Hooper, the scared slave boy, going nowhere.

The next day it was harder to go on. His punctured legs hurt, his stomach growled, his head pounded, and his brain worked slowly.

Toward dark he caught up with a party of gold-seekers who had camped for the night. They nodded and said, "Evening," in reply to his greeting. But they were watching him, nudging one another, and whispering. At last one of them, a skinny fellow with hair so blond it was nearly white, called, "Come over here, boy. We want to talk to you."

Jonas approached warily. "Evening, sir."

The man was picking his teeth with a toothpick. He drawled, "Your name Jonas?"

Jonas was too stunned to reply.

"Because if it is, your master's looking for you. He paid a man to ride up the line and tell people he'd give them a nice reward for bringing you back."

"M—my name ain't Jonas. It be Quincy. Quincy Benson."

The man shrugged lazily. "Well, Quincy or Jonas or whoever you are, you need to hide out for a while. Now, me and most of my men are from Kansas Territory and we don't hold with slavery. If you like, you can take supper with us and hide in our wagon."

Jonas thought. What if the man was lying? What if he and his party planned to deliver him to Master Percy and collect the reward themselves? On the other hand, the man might be telling the truth. And the coffee and pot of beans smelled awfully good.

"My name ain't Jonas," he repeated slowly, "and I ain't no slave. I been taking a message up the line for my boss, Mr. Tate. I got a mite lost, though, and I be plenty tired. If I could have a bite of supper and a quick nap in your wagon, I'd be much obliged."

"Help yourself." The man swept a hand to indicate the supper that was cooking. "My name's Horace Bratton. These are my men. We're headed to the gold fields."

Jonas shook hands all around, looking each man straight in the eye, and took the tin plate and cup the men gave him. He was disappointed to find that the coffee was old and the beans were so bad he would have been ashamed to offer them to a mule.

But after he'd eaten, his brain worked better.

I never should have trusted that shifty-eyed Bratton fellow, he thought. I got to run, but I got to be careful. If he knows I aim to run, he might tie me up.

He thanked Mr. Bratton for the meal and offered his help washing the dishes.

"Nah, you go on in the wagon and have your nap," the man said. He smiled, showing crooked, yellow teeth. "After all, you're our guest."

"Thank you kindly, sir."

Jonas found a bed in the wagon. It looked awfully comfortable, with its thin mattress and pile of wool blankets. He lay down, holding his flour sack close, but he didn't dare fall asleep. If he did, he might wake up looking into the smug, fish face of Master Percy.

He knew his fears were justified when, after dark, he heard low voices coming from behind the wagon.

"Just looked in at the boy. He's fast asleep."

"Didn't suspect a thing, did he?" There was a low chuckle. "Good thing his owner thought to hire a rider to bring the message up the line."

"Shall we hogtie the boy and carry him back to his owner, or go fetch his owner and bring him here?"

"I'm for going to fetch his owner. It'd be easier that way."

"That's what I think, too, Horace."

"All right, then. The guards will be on duty soon. They'll watch the wagon tonight and make sure he doesn't escape. Then, first thing in the morning, I'll go looking for his owner. We'll split the one-hundred-dollar reward."

Jonas didn't wait to hear more. He got up and found his flour sack, then crept to the front of the wagon. Silently he climbed down and ran into the night.

11

JONAS RAN FOR A LONG TIME. THEN HE STOPPED, OUT OF breath. He was lost. Had he run straight out from the trail or slantwise to it? He didn't know. He didn't know how far he had run, either. When he left the wagon, there had still been a slight paleness to the western sky, but now it was gone and he didn't remember where it had been. The whole sky was dark. There was a moon, but it was just one of those little old thumbnails.

Panic built up inside him until he thought he'd start hollering like a crazy boy. He tried to think what Mr. Quincy or Sky would do if they were lost out here at night. Well, of course, Mr. Quincy knew too much about the trail to get into such a predicament. As for Sky, she'd be practical-minded. She'd figure out something that made sense, based on what she'd learned from her books. But Jonas hadn't yet learned anything that would help. Or had he? He searched his mind for a bit of knowledge he could use.

Suddenly he looked at that skinny little moon again. If the sun set in the west, wouldn't the moon do the same? He decided he'd watch it for a while. If it kept sinking lower, it must be setting. If Jonas faced it, he would be facing west, and the trail would have to be somewhere to his left. If the trail were to his right, he reasoned, he would have crossed the river already.

Soon he was certain that the moon was creeping down toward the horizon. He was proud of himself for figuring out where west was. At the same time, he was kind of sorry he'd been right: it meant that the moon would soon disappear over the horizon. Once its friendly glimmer was gone, the night would be as dark as the inside of a grave. The stars wouldn't help him. Tate had talked about something called the North Star, but Jonas had no idea which one of those twinkling specks it might be.

He decided to head back toward the trail before the moon disappeared. He'd have to be watchful so he didn't run into the Bratton gang, but he had no wish to spend the night lost on the plains of Kansas Territory.

The eerie howl of a wolf sent him scurrying.

It had been getting cooler ever since he'd left Mr. Bratton's wagon, and now a chilly wind breathed down his neck. He put on his extra shirt. His coat would have been mighty welcome, but it was back in the Chalmerses' wagon.

By the time Jonas saw the white canvas wagon tops of a wagon train camp, his teeth were chattering and he was hugging himself to try to get warm. He looked over the camp, and was certain it wasn't Mr. Bratton's. Thank you, Lord, he thought. He had come back to the Santa Fe Trail.

He walked down the trail a ways to where no wagon trains were camped, and there he crossed the wide, rutted trail and headed over to the Arkansas River banks. Once he was hidden in the bushes by the riverside, he felt safe enough to rest. He was so tired he could hardly stay awake, but even when he curled up tight he shivered uncontrollably from the cold. He got up and began walking west again, stumbling and half dreaming with fatigue.

When he heard a flute playing faintly in the distance, he thought he was back at Split Oak Farm, listening to Tate. The song was an odd, tuneless one—wild and haunting. It went on and on, seeming to lead him through the night.

"Follow the music, Jonas," he heard Tate's voice saying. "You want to get to that free land, you got to follow the music. Ain't no other way to get there."

A cold gust of wind startled him out of his dream. Tate was dead, he remembered, and he was in Kansas Territory. The flute playing was coming not from the field hands' quarters at home but from an Indian camp up ahead.

Jonas knew he ought to be scared, but he felt drawn to that camp. There would be people and food, and, best of all, a campfire and warm blankets. The Indians wouldn't give him back to Master Percy, either. No, they'll just scalp me, is all, he thought. But he couldn't help feeling as if Tate was speaking to him through that flute song.

He walked into the camp. The flute player was still playing, inside one of the tipis. Two Indian men were sitting outside by the fire, and they stood up when they saw him. He recognized them as the men who had ridden past him on their ponies the night before. One had a broad, craggy face, with smooth black hair parted in the middle, a stern mouth, and piercing eyes. The other had a smoother, gentler face, and his hair was tied in long braids. Both men looked surprised and curious, but not hostile or wrathful.

"Evening," Jonas said warily. Part of him was thinking he must be out of his mind, and the other part was just longing to sit down by that campfire.

The men nodded to him and murmured something that sounded like "How, how." To Jonas's relief, the broad-faced one indicated the campfire and then pointed to him, making it clear as day that he was welcome to sit down.

"Thank you, sir," Jonas said gratefully, and fairly collapsed beside that fire. He didn't think anything had ever felt as good as the warmth that spread across him.

The men exchanged brief words, and the one with the gentle look went into the tipi that the flute music was coming from. The tune stopped, and an Indian boy who appeared to be about Jonas's age followed the man out. He had a countenance similar to the man's, and wore his hair tied back from his face. He still carried the flute in his hands.

"How do you do," he said to Jonas in careful English. "I am Yellow Bird. Welcome to our camp. My father, Clever Hawk, told me you are here."

At first Jonas was too astonished to do anything but stare. He remembered his manners and stood up. "Thank you. I be Jonas Quincy Benson. Hope I ain't pestering you none."

"Please, sit down. We will have the women bring you food."

"Oh, no!" Jonas cried. "Don't be waking them up for me. It ain't right."

But soon two women were bustling around, fetching and heating up food. One, who was young and shy, came over to put a huge, furry buffalo robe around Jonas. When he tried to thank her, she giggled and ran away.

"That is my sister, Little Antelope," Yellow Bird said.

The older woman, who had a kind, patient face, brought him a bowl of hot soup and dried berry cake. He thanked her and lit into the food with a passion. The soup was made of buffalo meat, corn, and a turnip-like vegetable, and both it and the cake were very pleasing to the taste. Yellow Bird watched Jonas eat, but didn't say anything. It struck Jonas as being thoughtful, to let him eat his fill and not interrupt with talk. If some strange boy had wandered into Master William's kitchen, he probably would have starved while people pestered him with questions.

When Jonas had finished eating and the women had cleared up the foodstuffs, Yellow Bird said, "You are out alone on a cold night."

Jonas figured that his comment was a polite way of asking him what his business was. He said, "I be looking for a friend who passed this way. A man named Jack Rulo."

"Jack Rulo!" Yellow Bird's face lit up. He turned and spoke rapidly to his father and the craggy-faced man, and they both smiled and nodded enthusiastically.

"We know Jack Rulo," Yellow Bird told Jonas. "All Arapaho know Jack Rulo. He helps us and trades fairly with us. If you are Jack Rulo's friend, you are our friend."

Excitedly Jonas asked, "Do you know where he is?"

Yellow Bird turned and talked to the two men again. Then he said firmly to Jonas, "Tomorrow we find Jack Rulo. Tonight you sleep."

Almost before Jonas knew what was happening, he was tucked up snugly under the buffalo robe inside Yellow Bird's family's tipi. His last waking thought was that he'd meant to tell Yellow Bird he'd had a friend back home who played the flute.

By the time Jonas woke up in the morning, news of his coming had spread throughout the camp. Outside the tipi, children waited to touch his skin, grab fistfuls of his hair, shriek, and giggle. Several women shooed them off and kept them away while Jonas ate a breakfast of boiled buffalo meat and a bowl of broth. He was afraid he was being greedy, but the women kept offering more, and he couldn't resist. For the last few days he had felt as if his stomach were sticking to his backbone.

Jonas had figured he and Yellow Bird would go look for Mr. Rulo. But when he had finished eating, Yellow Bird came to him holding a piece of tanned hide, a mussel shell full of red paint, and a smooth stick.

"I must hunt buffalo with the men," he said. "My brother, Sees Badger, will find Jack Rulo. Sees Badger speaks no English, but he can take Jack Rulo a message."

He set the writing materials on the ground beside Jonas and sat down to wait. The children, and even a few grown-ups, clustered around and watched eagerly.

Jonas put the tanned hide on his lap and dipped the stick into the red paint. But the alphabet letters had flown right out of his head. He couldn't think of how to make even one. Thank goodness, he thought, he still had the alphabet list Sky had made for him. He pulled it out of his pocket—and found that the letters were nothing but blurs of black ink. The paper must have gotten soaked when he had sat in the river to bathe his cactus wounds.

Think! he told himself. If you sit here all day, there ain't no way that boy can find Mr. Rulo.

Finally a letter came into his memory: a tall, proud letter with a little fishhook at the bottom. His own letter, *J*! He drew one on the hide, and heard a murmur of approval. The *O* was easy enough to remember. The *N* took some thought, but the *A* and the *S* were once again clear in his mind. As he made the S, he remembered the day in the wagon when Sky had first pointed out that snaky-looking letter on the salt sack.

Now JONAS stood out in bright red letters.

What else could he say? He thought of all the words he'd learned to read—tea, beans, and so on. There was only one that would serve the purpose. Slowly he wrote COME. Then he added PLEEZ. He wasn't sure he was spelling it right, but Mr. Rulo would understand.

"Good," said Yellow Bird, nodding. After the paint had dried, he rolled up the hide and handed it to a much younger boy. He told Jonas, "Sees Badger will find Jack Rulo and give him your message."

Sees Badger looked about Jigsy's age.

Jonas burst out, "Yellow Bird, are you sure that little boy can find Mr. Rulo?"

Yellow Bird looked surprised. "He will find Jack Rulo. He is named for an ancestor who saw a badger from far away, before anyone else could see it." He smiled. "My brother has the same good eyes."

Jonas nodded, but still he would have felt better if someone older were going.

Sees Badger mounted a pretty brown pony and rode away, carrying the hide bearing Jonas's message. Soon afterward most of the boys and men got on their horses and set out on the hunt. Yellow Bird waved to Jonas as they rode off.

The day seemed to stretch on forever. Jonas taught some of the Arapaho youngsters to say a few words in English, and he learned to say a few Arapaho words in return. He wrote A, B, and C in the dirt with a stick, just as Sky had once done for him, and then the children taught him to play a stick-and-hoop game.

He kept glancing nervously toward the trail, hoping to see a little boy and a big bear-man riding into the camp. This was Sunday, he thought. Mr. Rulo and his train would be preparing for the Jornada del Muerto. Maybe he wouldn't have time to come, or maybe Sees Badger wouldn't live up to his name. Anyway, Jonas reminded himself, there was no guarantee that Mr. Rulo would help him.

As he was finishing his lunch of buffalo soup, a cry went up and several excited children came running over. "Jack Rulo! Jack Rulo!" they cried.

Jonas quickly set down his bowl and got up just as Sees Badger proudly rode into camp with Mr. Rulo following.

"Jonas, what happened? Where's Jeremiah?" Mr. Rulo asked.

Jonas told him his friend had been shot. "Mr. Quincy will be okay," he assured the big man quickly. "Thank you mightily for coming. Thank you, too, Sees Badger!"

The boy returned his smile and led his pony away. Mr. Rulo dismounted and tied up his buckskin horse.

"Tell me what's going on, Jonas," he said.

Jonas told him the story in as simple a fashion as he could, leaving out some of the details. Even so, Mr. Rulo looked perplexed and broke in with questions more than once.

When Jonas was finished, Mr. Rulo said slowly, "Now, let me see if I got this straight—Jeremiah's been shot up but he'll recover, the doctor sent you off with the three nincompoops that were responsible, you escaped and nearly got caught again and wandered into the Arapaho camp, you can't go home for reasons you'll tell me later, and you aimed to go to Canada but now you can't because Jeremiah ain't going to California on account of getting shot."

"Yes, sir. I reckon that sums it up. But there be one thing I ain't told you yet." Jonas took a deep breath. "Since I can't get to Canada, I was hoping maybe you'd take me—that is, I was hoping I could work my way—on your train down to that land of Mexico. The doctor's gal, Sky, she say she think I could be free there."

He was looking straight into Mr. Rulo's face, but he couldn't begin to guess what the thoughts in that matted head might be.

Finally Mr. Rulo said flatly, "So you want to go with my train down to Mexico."

"Yes, sir."

"Jonas, I know I've said more than once that I'd be happy to have you. But—well, dang it, do you know what you're asking?"

So Mr. Rulo didn't want him, after all. Jonas hung his head. Then he thought, I ain't giving up yet. Raising his chin, he said, "All I know is that one time Mr. Quincy said you could always be counted on."

"He did, did he?" A ghost of a grin lurked behind those black whiskers.

"Yes, sir. And because of that, I been walking and starving and freezing, trying to find you. I got my heart set on getting free. If you don't want me going to Mexico with you, I'll find me another Santa Fe–bound train I can go with."

Mr. Rulo shook his big head. "Jonas, you mistook my meaning! I didn't say I don't want you. I just wanted to make sure you know what you're in for. It's a long, hard trip. There's too much sun, and too many Indians, and too little water. You'll have a tough job cooking for me and my crew, and some of the boys may give you a rough time. I can't pay you, either."

"I don't care about pay, sir! I just want to get to freedom." Jonas hesitated. "I will be free once I get to Mexico, won't I?"

"Sure as I'm standing here. Those Mexicans don't like slavery."

"Then," said Jonas, "that's where I want to go, and if you'll have me, I want to go with your train."

"Of course I'll have you. Why, your cooking'll have every mule skinner in the West wanting to work for me! Besides, you strike me as having plenty of grit and spunk."

The men and boys came riding into camp, home from the day's buffalo hunt. They all shook hands with Mr. Rulo, and they treated Sees Badger as a hero for finding him. To everyone's delight, Mr. Rulo gave them pouches of coffee and tobacco, which he had brought in his saddle-bags.

Then, while Jonas was saying goodbye to Yellow Bird and hearing about the hunt, Mr. Rulo walked off with Clever Hawk. When he returned, he was holding the reins of a spotted, bright-eyed pony.

"Here you go," he said, handing the reins to Jonas. "I just bought you a horse."

"A *horse*? But, sir, I ain't never ridden a horse before!"

"Well, then it's time you got started. A man that works for me needs a horse."

Mr. Rulo mounted his buckskin, and Jonas clambered awkwardly onto his new pony.

"Let's head out," Mr. Rulo said, raising a hand in farewell to the Arapaho.

As Jonas bounced after Jack Rulo on the spotted pony, he knew he made a sorry sight. He didn't blame the children for laughing at him.

But, he figured, he had learned to read and write. He guessed he could learn to ride a pony, too. Besides, what did it matter if people laughed or if he felt as if he were straddling a barrel? He was heading to freedom!

AUTHOR'S NOTE

In 1858, American newspapers carried exciting news: gold had been discovered in the Rocky Mountains! Many people were sure they could make their fortunes if they could get to the Rockies. The best place to look, they were told, was near Pikes Peak, in what is now Colorado but was then western Kansas Territory—or "K.T." There, the newspapers said, you could find gold wherever you dug.

In the spring of 1859, thousands of gold seekers, including many from Missouri, set out across the prairie. The May 6, 1859, issue of the *Liberty Tribune* of Liberty, Missouri, stated: "A Nebraska newspaper says that slavery is already established in the Pike's Peak region—that the Mexicans are there with peons, and that Southerners are on their way there with slaves, from every Southern State."

Even though Kansas Territory—and later, the state of Kansas—was free, those Southerners probably didn't worry about their slaves escaping. For one thing, slaves who went to K.T., or to any other free state or territory, were still legally considered slaves. Their masters could cross the border to find them, or hire professional slave catchers to search for them and bring them back in chains.

Besides, surely no slave would try to escape in that vast, unexplored wilderness! The strange western land bred wolves and rattlesnakes; it offered little water; and it was home to the Kaw, Pawnee, and Arapaho people, whose ways were unfamiliar and frightening to the gold seekers. How terrifying the journey must have been to a slave who could not read, had no firearms, knew nothing about geography, and had never traveled more than a mile or two from home.

Still, there were slaves desperate enough to try escaping any way they could. Even though most runaway slaves headed to Canada, some—particularly those in Texas—fled to Mexico. In 1855, it was estimated that up to five thousand fugitive slaves had entered that country. The government of Mexico declared that slaves were free once they crossed the Rio Grande, and refused to sign a treaty promising to return them to the United States.